DEATHGATE

BY SCOTT ANTHONY TAYLOR

Published by

The S.A. TAYLOR COMPANY
Copyright © 2011

Dedicated to

My best friend…
Who I am so lucky to be married to.
Thanks baby for your patients, tolerance,
understanding, and love.

Many waters cannot quench the flame of
love, neither can the floods drown it.

Song of Solomon 8:7

Special Thanks To

The Striking Viking, the greatest dive instructor
(And his beautiful bride)

Patrick and Jacqueline Carmack
and Peggy Schwartz
Our angels on earth

CHAPTERS

Act I

Act II

Act III

Characters

Thank you for joining me through a recollection of the miraculous love and works of the Almighty God in the lives of two of His children.

On this journey you will be privy to one of the most rare of mortal experiences; a window into the spiritual, an immortal perspective of an event in the physical world.

You will walk through events as seen by eyes of flesh, in front of the curtain on the stage of life. In our story you will also get a glimpse of the divine stagehands that work the unsung invisible.

It is my pleasure to present to you, *Deathgate*.

Then I looked and behold a [*gateway*] standing open in heaven....
Revelation 4:1

SCOTT ANTHONY TAYLOR

A GATEWAY

There is a place… a place between the spiritual realm of heaven and the physical realm on earth.

A barren place…lifeless.

It has hosted innumerable, epic battles throughout the eons of time.

Battles against the forces of heaven and hell.

A place claimed by Lucifer, although not given to him.

The heavenly hosts must pass through this space to reach the children of man in the physical realm.

Countless messengers of God have been ambushed and battled against here by the demons of Lucifer.

One such battle is written of in the old testaments of God.

Michael, the arc angel, was sent by the King of Glory to earth to tell His servant Daniel that his prayer was answered. On his way, a legion of Lucifer's fallen broke out with such forceful engagement that even Michael was delayed in his assignment.

The battle waged for twenty-one days before Michael was able to claim victory and fulfill his mission.

This nameless space between spaces, this battlefield of good and evil, is the realm of the gateways.

Gateways are ordained transitional passageways created by God.

They are a supernatural connection between heaven and earth, physical and spiritual, mortal and immortal.

As the children of Adam walk the path ordained by Almighty God, they will undoubtedly face many gateways.

Some seen, some felt, some heard, some asked.

Some require action of the smallest movement such as grabbing someone's hand, beaming a smiling, taking a step, or giving a compassionate embrace.

Others can take much more physical action.

They take the soul through an event that will cleanse away some of the grime left by the sinful nature.

As the grime is removed, not only can God be seen more clearly, but the soul is released from the burden and weight of it.

This was explained in the writings of the second book to the Corinthians. For the glory given mortals to walk in this day is not the glory planned for them tomorrow.

A Gateway takes the child of God closer to his Creator, a higher level of glory.

Every step that is granted to mortals to come closer to God is monumental. It is a movement that can only take place by God's grace and mercy.

It is a time of celebration but also a time of great concern and alertness. Each gateway is created for a specific mortal for a specific time.

When passed through, each gateway dramatically changes the path of the intended.

If not used by the mortal of whom it was ordained in the time allotted, its power ceases.

It becomes a lifeless marker of missed divine opportunity. Lucifer then makes it an altar of victory for his kingdom.

God's saints are most vulnerable during these events.

It is also when Lucifer attempts to disrupt and corrupt the gateway to deter the saints from passing through.

Although a gateway is a supernatural spirit realm event, the effects of it can be felt even seen, in the physical realm. The unnatural intrusion into the physical realm causes nature to react unpredictably.

On rare occasions where there is an overcast sky, one might be fortunate enough to see a hole tearing through the clouds and brilliant rays of what would appear to be sunlight streaming down.

This phenomenon could very well be a gateway in progress.

Nature, being abruptly intersected with the supernatural, responds by altering its own laws and submits to the priority of God's divine intervention.

This tear in the clouds is in fact the reaction of nature as the Gateway plunges into the realm of the physical.

The streams that appear to be sunlight actually are light from the Majesty of Heaven breaking through the realms escorting the angels and guardians onto the physical earth.

Gateways take on many shapes.

Some look immense but are actually very thin. Once it has been decided and determined to walk through, the transition is quick and is completed as swiftly as it appeared.

Some are thick and have the appearance more like a tunnel than a gate.

These can be rough, made of uneven ground, full of objects to stumble on and holes to fall into.

They are always angled upward so that through the toil of pitfalls there is the constant strain of climbing.

Many children of the Almighty will discover on their path several gateways lined up one after another, each a bit different.

No matter what is found on the path of the righteous, the divine Master of the Universe will provide all that will be needed to successfully pass through.

The enemy, from useless stones or "baggage" that the mortal is dragging along with him, constructs false gateways.

These stones can be hurts, unforgiveness, fear, bitterness, false truth, or anger picked up along the journey of life.

These false gateways are built as traps and snares to deter the saint from his ordained path. But none can be constructed without the permission of the Almighty God. For the Lord of hosts, your merciful God, has set many laws into the foundations of eternity.

One such law is that anything placed on a ordained path of His children, even though it be built for destruction or calamity, becomes a step of upward illumination and edification.

Like all divinely commissioned gateways, it too removes another fragment of their corruptible heart so that His Spirit may expand in them.

There is another gateway that takes the spirit and the body beyond its natural limits. This gateway is not merely one of soul passage nor one of just conscious decision. This gateway separates the soul from the body.

This not only elevates the soul closer to God, but it also determines if the soul will stay in the physical realm.

It is the most serious and dangerous of the gateways. To successfully pass through this gate, it takes immense planning and protection from the immortal.

Lucifer and his fallen angels double their efforts in attempt to keep the soul from returning to its physical body. This life-altering gateway is called,

a Deathgate...

The Overture

Place of Reflection

As I turning westerly down the sandy footpath, the wind began to blow harshly.

The path curved through heavy, thorny brush and viny foliage.

Grabbing the ends of my jacket, I attempted to zip it up. The fierce gusting wind battled my attempt, but finally success was mine and I zipped it to my neck.

"I can't believe how chilly and gray it is here," I thought.

Four hours earlier I was sweating in the bright, cloudless sky wearing only a t-shirt and shorts. Now it was 50 degrees cooler and no longer blue sky.

Driving towards the coast earlier that day, it seemed as if there were an invisible wall separating two distinct climates. Passing through the invisible barrier, the climate and landscape changed abruptly.

I was told that this is called a "marine layer".

DEATHGATE

It was as if God drew a line and proclaimed that beyond this point would be a different land.

This land will have thick gray clouds and fog. The fog was so heavy that I couldn't see where I had started down the path from the dirt parking lot.

Having lived in Michigan for the majority of my life, I had seen a lot of crazy weather.

Now, deep into the marine layer, it had a feel of autumn.

I loved the fall.

It felt comforting and cozy.

The type of weather that gives an urging to find an old overstuffed leather chair next to a crackling fire, to read a classic novel, and to sip some hot cider.

Pressing forward, I glanced over at the foliage along the trail. It had become somehow uniform.

It was still very overgrown and thick but it was the same kind of greenery. Looking closer, spots of deep red could be seen throughout the viny brush.

"Raspberries!" I exclaimed.

I stopped, bent down and picked a couple especially dark ones. They were sweet and juicy.

I reached down again, grabbed another handful and continued to press forward.

A little farther down the path, a crashing sound was heard softly mingled in the wind.

It was rhythmic and continued to get louder the farther down the trail I walked.

SCOTT ANTHONY TAYLOR   15

DEATHGATE

The sandy path got steadily narrower and steeper.

Soon it veered to the left around a large rocky outcropping. Beyond the rocks it turned right and abruptly ended at the top of a small cliff.

Below the cliff was a beach and the turbulent ocean.

The grayish green-blue water rushed toward the shore with white-capped waves crashing on the rocky shoreline.

This scene stretched out to the north and south as far as the eye could see.

These waters were unfamiliar to me.

The ocean I was used to was the tropical kind.

The kind that is of pristine aqua marine, nearly transparent waters that lap up gently onto white powder beaches.

These rough waters were of fabled stories told of great white whales and pirates sailing ships along the coast looking for secret caves to hide their plunder.

In spite of all the harshness of the landscape and weather, it was beautiful.

The smell was very fragrant.

The mingled aroma of fish, seaweed, and salt all danced in the heavy westerly wind that had blown in from thousands of miles and lands unknown.

It generated a warm sensation in the innermost part of my soul.

Dozens of movies had been shot in this area.

It was obvious why.

Looking down from the cliff, I noticed what appeared to be a makeshift path wandering down to the beach below.

I turned around and started backing down through the jagged rocks. It didn't take long to realize that this really wasn't a trail but a path of least resistance.

Halfway down, a sobering thought hit me,

"I will have to climb back up this way!"

"Oh well, too late now," I chuckled to myself.

One final stretch down and my foot landed on the beach.

I looked up with a sense of pride at the much taller than I thought cliff that I just mastered.

Taking a couple of deep breaths and wiping the perspiration from my forehead, I turned again toward the now roaring ocean.

Taking another deep breath, this time of relaxation, I headed towards the water's edge.

This was much different from any beach I had been on.

Even the sand was unique.

It was very dark, even black in some places. Not fine, but kind of rough and more like tiny pebbles.

The water's edge was outlined by large outcroppings of rock, some protruding out like towers.

As I continued to scan the beautiful sight, I noticed the fascinating tide pools. Small miniature oceans trapped in carved out sections of rocks. Each pool teamed with colorful life, beautiful sea anemones, tiny fish, starfish and little crabs.

Suddenly a deep screeching noise was heard coming from just off shore.

A large rock grouping hosted several sea lions frolicking among themselves.

A satisfactory smile grew across my face as I contemplated the unexplainable love I had for the water.

I loved everything to do with the water from boating and swimming to kayaking and, of course, scuba diving… my ultimate passion.

I loved the life below the surface.

There is incredible peace underwater.

I found myself craving the experience.

It is an entirely different world. It is like a euphoric drug.

I became hypnotized standing there watching the rhythmic crashing of the waves over and over again.

Walking closer to the water, I noticed a tingling in my stomach.

At first I thought it was just excitement.

This wasn't an excitement tingle; it was an uneasy one. Reaching the water's edge it hit me,

"It has been a year since I have been to the water."

Slowly feelings of anger, fear, hurt, and even resentment pushed into my mind.

Resentment that something I loved so much would hurt someone I loved even more.

It had been a year since the accident.

I thought the intense feelings had faded away by now.

Being on the water again evoked all kinds of emotions of the past.

My mind began to toss in turmoil, like the surging surf.

Memories suppressed, gushed to the surface.

My mind followed suit with bombardments of

"Why…?"

"What if…?"

"If only…!"

It is amazing that an event lasting the span of a few minutes could impact a life so dramatically.

"Life is so fragile," I whispered.

That incident marked the beginning of a new path in life that changed me emotionally, mentally, and spiritually.

The memories flooded in as I began to walk though the events of the past…

Act I

The Immortal

God, The Master Playwrite, has laid out the acts and scenes of His children's lives. These writings contain notes of instruction to the heavenly hosts for their parts in each act and transition.

On one particular day, Almighty God sent out a proclamation throughout the realm of paradise to summon the hosts, angels, and guardians involved in a new chapter from the Book of Life; a chapter written before time began and would now physically come to pass.

"The opening of a new chapter in the book of Scott and Darnisha Taylor is now at hand.

Convene at the reading room in the palace of God."

The message floated throughout the vastness and spectacular magnitude that is paradise like a feather on the wind only heard by those whom God willed.

Paradise…can words even begin to describe it to finite minds?

You see, in the spiritual realm all the senses are magnified including those unable to be used in the physical world.

A communion and communication exists beyond the primitive verbal; an innate, spiritual connection with all things. An intimate understanding that all things are truly alive and engaged in praise and worship to the Creator.

Although beyond imagination, paradise is not all that unfamiliar.

It is easy to see the influences in the physical realm that the Creator emulated from His spiritual home. The many landscapes of the planet earth are descendants from the epic expressions of a Creator proud of His creation.

The very notable differences between the two are the absence; even utter unawareness, of decay, deterioration, corrosion, and death. The human mind is oblivious to what these elements of sin have had not only on the human condition, but also on the earthly creation.

The landscape of Paradise is perfect in its completeness. The golden fields of the flat lands flow seamlessly into majestic mountains with singing crystal waterfalls. The waterfalls feed into mountain streams that make their way into the forests of lush green vegetation and towering trees so entrancing that a physical mind cannot process it all.

Age of vegetation in paradise does not add size but depth and intensity.

Imagine, the beauty of a single flower that is tens of thousands of years old.

The center of all of heaven, the heart of Paradise, is the city of the Living God.

This is where His glowing palace is planted with roots stretching deep into the fabric of eternity.

The tower can be seen throughout all of paradise shimmering as an eternal beacon giving life to all creation.

The palace hosts countless halls, cathedrals, and courtyards. The library of the Book of Life, in the center of the palace, has the most activity.

Though the Book of Life is a single book, it has countless volumes. In these volumes are found the life and times of each of the children of God.

Bordering the library are numerous smaller halls called reading rooms.

In these rooms, the keeper of the book of life brings out one chapter at a time to be read to all the hosts and assigned angels.

These rooms are breathtakingly beautiful.

They are oval in shape; each illuminated by shimmering iridescent pearled walls.

The walls curve upward and inward overhead. They stop to leave an opening where the roof would be and are trimmed by a massive rose quartz molding. The molding is elaborately carved and accented with precious stones.

The remainder of what would be a domed ceiling is completely open.

The throne room of the Living God is elevated high above the center of the palace in a glowing tower. This was crafted so that the Almighty God could be present in every reading room.

The guardians of Scott and Darnisha where excited as they responded to the call of Almighty God. The couple had recently finished their chapters as singles and just entered into their chapters that God had written for their new life together.

An unusually large number of angels from other realms were present for this event.

It made the guardians of the Taylors', Enoch and Israfel, a bit nervous.

"What is going on?"

Israfel asked as she looked around the room trying not to stare at the unexpected attendees.

"I don't have any idea," Enoch, Scott's guardian replied,

"I just assumed it would be a normal post-wedding reading for us to assist them in the relationship transition. But this is far beyond that."

Enoch was from the guardian clan of writers and visionaries, creators of things unseen. He helped in the inspiration of new ideas.

He was a deep thinker and always very aware of the beauty of his surroundings. He was prepared to inspire and equip children of God with new ideas and vision at a moment's notice.

His inspiring appearance itself created images in the mind of exciting visionary endeavors and things yet to be created.

Attached to a strap that Enoch carried over his shoulder was a square bag.

Under the flap of the bag was a shimmering silver quill. In the bag was a notebook of ancient parchment paper, one quarter of it full of notes, thoughts, ideas, and drawings.

Israfel, Darnisha's guardian, was from the clan of worshipers. Israfel was an angel of music and inspirer of worship songs to the Lord.

Her appearance was as if music itself took form.

Melodies flowed from her long gown and sparkling hair as she walked.

This was a trait all in this clan have as did their clan leader, Lucifer, before his fall into darkness.

She carried with her a small harp that David, the writer of the Psalms, fashioned just for her.

The pair were especially nervous concerning the presence of three centurion angels. Elemeniah, Azariel, and Sachiel from the commanding legion of wind and water.

Sachiel was the presiding commander over all waters. Elemeniah watched over those who travel on waters. Azariel ruled over the winds.

They were awesome in their appearance, huge in stature. The formality of their actions and speech was intimidating because they spoke with the sound of rushing wind and crashing waves.

Across the room standing stoically alone was Barakiel, the angel of financial wisdom and success. Barakiel wore two sashes that criss-crossed his chest. Each sash held a large ancient book; one book of worldly favor, the other of worldly wisdom. The sashes sparkled brilliantly as the lights of the room reflected off the encrusted gold and rainbow-colored jewels. He seemed to be illuminated thus unintentionally drawing the focus of the room.

Flying in were three more guardians unfamiliar to this group. As they entered the meeting area they announced loudly, "We are Vohumanah, Shemael , and Gavreel the guardians of the children Carmack and Schwartz. We have been summoned by the Lord!"

Enoch and Israfel greeted them as they introduced themselves.

Vohumanah introduced herself first as the guardian of the woman Jacqueline. Vohumanah was from the clan of encouragement. This clan assists in transforming negative thoughts and worries into a positive and optimistic outlook . Her bubbly energetic personality corresponded perfectly with her appearance that seemed to emanate positive energy of excitement and anticipation.

She then introduced Shemael who was Patrick's guardian, Jacqueline's husband. Shemeal was from the clan of inspirers of thankfulness and gratitude. Gavreel then stepped forward and introduced herself as Jacqueline's best friend Peggy's guardian. Gavreel's air and mannerisms gave away the fact she came from the peacemaker's clan.

The new trio and the Taylor's duo soon began sharing their questions of the meeting.

Then a euphoric presence fell on the crowd. A sweet scent of jasmine and lavender swirled around the room.

Aneal appeared gently descending through the opening of the room's ceiling. Everyone breathed a sigh.

Aneal was the archangel of passion and romance. She was breathtakingly beautiful. Her long hair flowed down her back and over her extremely form-fitting gown. She was always greeted with raised eyebrows wherever she went, especially from the female angels.

As the angels from each side of the new union shared thoughts of their divine destiny, a trumpet blast was sounded.

The massive doors of the library began to open. Brilliant light raced through the opening of the great doors as well as cherubim's singing songs of praise and adoration to Most High God.

Then through the magnificent light walked Jophiel the keeper of the Book of Life.

The proclamation angel announced him as he stepped forward with the new chapter, a complete book itself. Jophiel placed the book on a golden pedestal that seemingly had grown out of the center of the translucent quartz floor.

"The word of the Lord as He has written!" Jophiel announced.

"Praise the Lord!", the proclamation angels sang out and all began to praise the Lord each in his own way.

Jophiel opened the book.

Shimmering sparkles of light flew out from under the cover.

Jophiel in his place behind the podium looked up at the attendees of the reading. Immediately, the great hall fell silent in anticipation and reverence.

Jophiel began to speak…

"My children, the Taylors' shall walk through a deathgate."

As those words were spoken the crowd gasped, then fell silent. The silence was immediately broken with frantic whispers throughout the hall from their guardians.

"A Deathgate?

Already?

They are not ready!"

Jophiel lifted his head again to face the fellowship.

He turned the page in the Taylor book to find multiple unbound sheets of sparkling parchment.

The ink on the inscriptions glistened in the light.

The parchments contained instructions, somewhat like stage notes.

He removed the parchments and handed them to the Proclaimer.

The Proclaimer then handed the parchment to each angel for whom it was written.

Now, Jophiel began to read the words of the book.

As he did, everyone in the hall knelt as the written words of the Lord filled the room like a refreshing mist.

The Lord's will was being proclaimed.

"...no permanent harm shall fall on either nor anything shall be lost, thus saith the Lord," were the final words Jophiel spoke completing the new chapter.

He then slowly closed the book.

Everyone in the hall shouted with great excitement and joy,

"Praise the Lord and the everlasting word of His will!"

The Proclamation swirled like smoke and slowly rose to the throne of God.

As God sanctified the meeting, each host left to fulfill his calling.

The first to take to the air were the centurions of wind and waters.

Their job would be to alter the very fabric of nature for the children of God.

Soon after, the guardians took flight and launched through the open roof, off to inspire their assigned people in the part they would play in this monumental event.

Dezro

The realm of the Gateways.

The battlefield of good and evil.

A place filled with remnants of ancient battles, shrines to battles won, and unfulfilled gateways never passed through now dead and crumbling.

A demon scout of Lucifer hides among the rubble close to the entrance of heaven.

He's there to eavesdrop, to hear something discussed by the angels and guardians leaving heaven and heading to fulfill their assignments on earth.

The demon scout inches closer to the immense gate leading into paradise.

The decrepit demon shields his eyes from the radiant glow spilling out from the realm of heaven.

As he tries to sneak closer yet, the overwhelming odor of sulfur and death alert the towering guardians with blazing swords on either side of the gate of his presence.

With the speed of a lightning strike, one of the guardians raised his sword and sliced through the rubble behind which the demon was hiding.

The flaming sword just missed the frail demon who scurried back on all fours to his original hiding hole like a rat.

Shaking and panting with fear, he reassured himself that this spot was good enough.

After catching his breath, he began again to listen intently for some information that would help his master's cause.

Many moments later, two guardians exited the gates of heaven deep in conversation.

They discussed what was revealed to them in the reading room.

The demon bent his ear towards this interesting conversation.

"I can't believe we are going to allow her to be taken by death. She is so excited about her faith and her small group that she hosts."

"People like her are so rare in that city. To be a single woman in a country that outlaws serving our Lord is rare indeed," said the guardian.

"Death seems to have that one covered. I need something big to bring back to my master," Dezro said to himself.

He had not come across any significant information that his master was gleeful in hearing for many, many decades. He was considered a wash-up, a has-been in the demonic scouting legions.

"I just need one great event to restore my graces with the master and show the others that I can still get in on the big jobs."

Just then he saw the wind and water centurions shoot through the gate of heaven headed straight to earth.

"Where are they going in such a hurry? I've got to find out what's happening."

Soon following the centurions was another guardian.

"That is the guardian of Darnisha the worshiper. I have seen her before. God is very fond of her.

I have heard that she has finally married. I wonder if it has something to do with that?"

As he watched the guardian pass overhead, he caught a glimpse of a shimmering parchment with his sinister beady eyes.

"Damn!" he hissed out loud, "They are going through a deathgate. This must be an important one for centurions to be involved. Oh, this is it! This is a big one!"

Dezro could hardly contain his excitement.

"My lord will be so pleased with me! Maybe he will even allow me back tormenting Christians on earth; no, let's not get ahead of ourselves now, Dezro. I need to get this to my master before anyone else hears word of this event."

He quickly slithered through the battle remains and made great haste to his master's realm.

Dezro, winded and drained, ran as fast as he could to the gates of the throne room of Lucifer.

Unlike the realm of heaven, there is no open access to the palace or the throne.

The towering and gruesome gatekeeper sneered at Dezro as he approached.

"My lord, my lord, I have great news."

"What is it, Dezro?" growled the gatekeeper behind the gate.

"Do you have some loser drug addict who is thinking of suicide? What ridiculously insignificant bit of information do you have that deems entrance to our most high lord?"

"A Deathgate, my lord."

"What?" replied the gatekeeper surprisingly.

"Yes, my lord, a Deathgate for the Taylors, Scott and Darnisha."

"Hmmm, sounds interesting. Why don't you just fill me in and I will tell our master."

"No!", shouted Dezro.

"I must tell him myself!"

With of look of disgust, the gatekeeper responded, "Very well, you shall enter."

Dezro's corroded black heart beat heavy with excitement.

"I cannot believe I am being allowed to enter the master's throne room! It has been centuries since I was last allowed in."

The gatekeeper growled at the guards on either side of the entrance.

With great effort, the guards slowly pulled the massive gates open for Dezro.

As they opened, the excitement of entering the master's throne room produced a single tear that fell down Dezro's scared putrid cheek.

With weak knees, Dezro wobbled through the gates and was met by the throne room announcer.

SCOTT ANTHONY TAYLOR   31

"I have not seen you before? What are you?"

"Your servant, my lord." Dezro bowed.

"We have met before. It has just been awhile since I have been allowed in."

"Hmmm," the announcer responded with an air of superiority.

"Your name?"

"Dezro, my lord. I am a scout for the master."

"Right, follow me, say nothing until you are announced and asked to speak."

The announcer, noticeably annoyed, turned and led Dezro down the dark hallway to the entrance of the throne room. He walked with great pomp into the cavernous sanctuary.

"My lord and prince of the air, the physical, and underworld, and heir to the throne of God himself, your lowly servant, scout Dezro!"

Dezro walked through the dark dank hall into the throne room of Lucifer. His legs shook and knees buckled as he stepped forward.

Immediately he felt the heat from the fires leaping and dancing in large stone caldrons. The caldrons lined the aisle on either side. They started at the entrance of the great hall and ended at the foot of Lucifer's throne.

The enormous throne was carved with images of worldly pleasure of flesh and self-edification, the foundations of his kingdom.

Music swirled around the massive hall, all originating from the angelic figure sitting upon his throne. The music praised the flesh and inspired thoughts of only pleasing oneself.

Dezro walked reverently down the aisle.

The flames began to mesmerized him as they changed colors seductively dancing in the caldrons. He felt the flames reaching deep within him engulfing him with burning lust.

As Dezro reached the steps to Lucifer's throne, he fell to his knees, head bowed humbly.

"Speak, servant", Lucifer spoke in a bored and disinterested tone.

"They are taking the Taylors through a Deathgate, my lord."

"A Deathgate?"

Lucifer echoed back in a hiss.

"We must stop this, my lord," spoke a deep, growling, female voice from the shadows alongside the throne.

"There is too much activity and celebration around this couple. We must do something."

From the deep shadows two beaming yellow eyes appeared and moved closer and closer until a black-cloaked figure could be seen.

It was Lucifer's companion, his minister, and confidant.

"The physical world scout overheard the couple talking about going scuba diving.

Let's attack them while they are in the water. Let's scar him, my lord. Let us physically harm him."

The master of the underworld, deep in thought slowly responded, "No, do nothing to him. I know this one well.

I have been allowed to torment his self-worth and plague him with insecurities for years.

Let us focus on her.

If we harm her, he will destroy himself over the guilt. Besides, I can't stand her worshipping God and her ability to usher His servants into His presence any longer.

I must silence her. Notify their tormentor. Instruct him to take a squad with him.

"My lord?"

Dezro softly interrupted.

Lucifer stopped and turned his attention annoyingly back towards Dezro and looked at him with disbelief.

"Please my Lord, let me have this assignment."

Lucifer's minister laughed mockingly but Lucifer remained silent.

"Surely, Dezro you jest! You are an impotent fool! You have been worthless to us for decades."

"Do you think you can handle this Dezro?" Lucifer calmly asked. "Yes, my lord, oh yes. I can destroy this couple. I have learned many things watching you work my lord."

"You can't be serious, my lord," Lucifer's confidant arrogantly responded.

"Silence!" Lucifer thundered.

"I will allow this, Dezro. I remember your work centuries ago in Rome; it was legendary"

Dezro, shocked that his master remembered his infamous work with the early Christians, lifted his head a little higher and inflated his chest.

"Thank you, my gracious lord. I will return with the news of their demise or I will not return."

"Very well Dezro. Go make havoc wherever you can. Look for an opportunity to end the flesh of the female. I will send a buffeter demon out ahead, quietly, to the lake Crystal that is where they are headed. Once it has accomplished its task, go Dezro and take a legion with you."

The Union of Two Books

Following divine instruction, Enoch touches Scott's thoughts...

Scott, standing in the master bathroom checking in the mirror to see if his goatee could use a trim, Enoch's suggestion materializes in Scott's mind.

"Babe," Scott called to his beautiful new bride who was putting on her shoes in the adjacent bedroom.

"What do you think about going up north for a day or two?"

"Oh, that would be great! Can we do it?" She replied excitedly.

"Sure, I will take off tomorrow and we can drive up to Crystal Lake. Maybe we can do a little scuba diving. We could even stay overnight in Traverse City. We can head back the next morning and get home in time to make the open houses we have to attend."

"Sure, that sounds great!" Darnisha replied.

"You don't have to dive if you don't want to," Scott assured his wife.

Darnisha was a diver but didn't share the love for it that he did.

Scott wanted to make sure she didn't feel obligated. For him, it was the main reason to go. He wanted to get one more dive in before the weather got too cold.

"No, I would like to go diving, too."

"OK, this will be great. Let me make sure I can get off work. It is kind of last minute, but I don't think it's a problem."

The couple loved going up to northern Michigan. It was one of the few perks of living in the state.

They especially enjoyed the Traverse area. It had been their favorite place to rest and enjoy the beauty of nature.

The past month had been quite eventful and exciting for the pair. The next day would be their three-week wedding anniversary.

For Scott it had been a challenging time.

Within the past year, he had sold the business that he started after being downsized from an executive management position.

The Michigan economy was in a bad state and it was very difficult to find work. Because of the bad economy and being ready for a new start together, the couple had been thinking about relocating. Their Pastor had just left to plant a church in Northern California. The couple really felt God leading them to go and help.

Over the past months, Scott had made several trips there looking for a new career opportunity.

So far he had found nothing.

After the last trip, he came back feeling very defeated. The couple decided to put the job search on hold until after their wedding so that the stress would not ruin the event.

The spiritual ceremony of the joining of two souls is even more divine and celebrated than the mortal counterpart.

All of heaven rejoices when two of God's children become one.

In the physical union of a man and woman there are a very rare few who have a deeper connection stemming from a deeper calling; a calling from an ordained union to fulfill a divine purpose for the kingdom of God.

This was the case of Scott and Darnisha's union.

The marriage celebration of Scott and Darnisha in heaven was more exciting than most because this wedding had many unusual aspects.

Darnisha held true to her vow of purity for 34 years, not only her virginity but any physical expressions to another man but her husband. Beyond her physical vow of purity was a deeper spiritual vow to her heavenly Father that was much greater than any physical expression.

That inner purity is what delighted the Father so greatly about Darnisha. She walked in a child-like faith that took a person of close relationship and true wisdom.

Since the angel in charge of music in heaven, Lucifer, was banished worship music must be created by God's children. So, God placed in Darnisha a seed from the tree of worship, which bares the fruit of new songs of praise to the Lord. Along with that seed, God gave Darnisha a voice that could penetrate the realm of heaven and directly access His throne.

He found great enjoyment and satisfaction listening to her as she sang new songs of worship to Him. The angels of heaven loved singing the songs she would write to her Savior.

Scott had a different journey.

Through a series of failure, rejection, disappointment, physical and mental complications, God established deep roots of character, patience, endurance and uncommon mercy.

God proved Himself loyal and able to sustain through any crisis of life Scott faced. Even through times that friends and family turned from him, God was there waiting with healing balm for the soul. Even healing for self-inflicted wounds caused by inaccurate perceptions and feeble attempts to fix something irreparable by mortal means.

God crafted for Scott a heart fashioned after His own Son; a heart of true compassion and grace. A heart that wanted to share all the pitfalls and hard lessons learned so others wouldn't have to walk the long road of recovery.

God blessed and gave favor to Scott and Darnisha's wedding in the physical realm.

The couple had a wonderful day celebrating their new union.

They planned the entire event together. It usually is the bride's domain, but Darnisha allowed Scott's input.

Their friends showered blessings on them.

Legendary gospel music singer, pastor and friend of Scott, gave the couple use of his beautiful church for their ceremony.

Several wonderful ladies from the couple's church prepared all the food and cakes for two receptions. Another friend did the wedding photos.

Still another produced their wedding video as a gift.

Scott's spiritual father sang and prayed a blessing over them.

Even the couple's pastor and his wife flew back from California to perform the ceremony.

Scott and Darnisha really wanted the wedding to represent what was important to them. They wanted it to have style and class.

Live jazz replaced the traditional wedding music throughout the entire event. The bridesmaids and groomsmen even sang at the end of the service as the couple greeted the guests.

The ceremony went perfectly.

The two receptions after the service were full of laughter, dancing, and endless hugs and kisses.

The menu included all of the couples' favorite gourmet dishes.

God even blessed them with a week at a condo just one mile from their favorite place, Walt Disney World, to act like kids again.

God's favor provided above and beyond everything Scott and Darnisha wanted for their special day.

To this day, the couple remains confounded and thankful for the amazing event that was provided by the generosity of God's loving people.

The Woman in Red

"Enjoy your afternoon."

The middle-aged Chinese woman spoke softly. There was a hint of anxiousness in her voice as she bowed to an elderly couple leaving the small restaurant after a late lunch.

As the door closed behind the couple, she turned to look at the large clock hanging at the rear of the restaurant.

"Just enough time to get home before my guests," she said to herself.

Quickly she made her way back to the elderly couple's table. Stacking the plates on her arm, she rushed them into the kitchen. She piled the plates into an old, very used stainless sink already filled with pans and dishes desperately needing cleaning.

The woman yelled out, "I am leaving now!" Having stayed over her scheduled time more than an hour.

"Make sure the dishes get washed soon."

"OK, see you tomorrow," came a voice from an adjacent room.

Glancing at the clock again, the woman walked briskly to the front door.

She grabbed her small handbag under a wooden stand by the door.

With bag in hand, the Chinese woman walked out the door onto the crowded sidewalk.

Taking a deep breath of not so fresh air, she launched herself into the human traffic packing the small space between the street and the endless wall of storefront buildings.

Beijing is a large city with an even larger population.

It is far from being known for its friendly streets.

The woman struggled to make headway past the coming foot traffic and beyond the slower walkers in front of her.

Fortunately, she lived only six blocks from here. It had been a bittersweet move to this extremely crowded, rundown part of town.

The middle-aged woman missed living in the country.

Sadly, she had to get a job in the city because of lack of work in the small village where she grew up.

With the four bus transfers she had to take every day to get home, it just made sense to move in closer to work.

The greatest benefit was meeting people in her apartment building that were having secret Bible studies.

This is how she met Jesus.

He changed her life.

And now, two years later, she was having her own meetings in her small apartment.

Her mind drifted to the night's events. The excitement of how the Holy Spirit was moving in her life made the stale, dirty air and crowded streets seem like a walk in a beautiful flower garden.

The church of God in Beijing was growing and on the move in spite of being outlawed.

Those caught in an unauthorized meeting were arrested, severely beaten, and sometimes killed.

But it didn't seem to affect the growth or deter believers from continuing to tell others of the love of Jesus.

The threat of getting caught and severely punished was real to her.

Just five months earlier, a small group gathering from her fellowship was raided.

The entire group was detained and separated. A few got away with back bruises from cane beatings. Two of them were never heard from or seen again.

Finally, after feeling as though for the last 30 minutes she had been in a pinball machine, she reached her apartment building.

It was tucked between two storefront shops down a narrow ally off a major street.

The small alley was full of people walking and riding bicycles. Scattered through the masses of people where vendors with small carts selling fresh fruits and vegetables.

There were no cars. A car couldn't get down this crowded alley even if someone tried.

The small old wooden door with dozens of layers of paint over could easily be missed.

On one side, a butcher shop full of dead chickens, ducks and other unknown species of animal were skinned and hanging on hooks from the ceiling.

On the other side, a fabric store was packed from floor to ceiling with shiny vibrant colored reams of cloth.

The woman loved this store.

She enjoyed sewing and making her own clothes like the beautiful red pantsuit she was wearing.

The woman, with all the force she could muster, pushed her body against the door.

The door unwillingly opened.

She quickly walked into the very narrow hallway and shut the door behind her in the same method she used to open it.

Walking forward in the dimly lit passage, the woman came to a very worn staircase. She ran up the stairs to another narrow hallway.

The first door on the left was her apartment.

She pulled her keys out of her small handbag and in one swift move stuck them in the lock, opened the door, and shut it behind her.

Turning two dead bolt locks on the door, the Chinese woman then turned the lamp on that was sitting on a small wooden table next to the door. Setting her keys and handbag down, she made a dash to the far side of her small one bedroom apartment to the tiny kitchen area.

The area was not much more than an oversized walk-in closet. The kitchen was made up of a tiny refrigerator, stove and a handful of cabinets.

The woman quickly turned on the stove, grabbed the teakettle and filled it with water from the small sink opposite the refrigerator. Setting the kettle on the stovetop she started straightning up her living / dining area.

In a matter of minutes, there was a knock on her door. Opening the door, she was greeted by three smiling faces.

They all said, "Hello," with a short bow followed by a long hug.

As they were hugging still in the hallway, four additional smiling faces appeared coming up the stairs and walking towards them. Joyous laughter flooded the tiny corridor. It was as if a long awaited family reunion was taking place. For them this excitement was experienced every week.

It was the woman's Bible study group.

Jackie

Spanning incomprehensible distance, Vohumanah rocketed out of the realm of heaven. Skillfully the guardian made her way into the realm of the physical dimension and to the planet earth.

Vohumanah continued her way across the northwestern hemisphere, over the lands called Michigan.

With determination and precision, she found a tall dark-haired woman named Jacqueline in a small settlement along a far eastern shore of a majestic lake.

Slowing down, Vohumanah effortlessly came to rest alongside her.

Jacqueline was sitting behind a long glass counter. It was full of beautiful one-of-a-kind handmade jewelry pieces created by Jacqueline herself.

Her shop was housed in one of the several quaint old buildings on the village's main street no more than four blocks long.

Jacqueline was sitting quietly looking out the large glass windows at the front of her shop onto the barren sidewalks of the village.

"Going to be a slow day today," Jacqueline said aloud to herself just as Vohumanah, her guardian, dropped an idea into her mind.

An image of a relaxing day fishing on the lake flashed into the middle-aged woman's thoughts.

It excited her spirit.

She decided to close up shop, finish up some errands, and try to talk her best friend Peggy into taking the boat out fishing with her.

Jacqueline quickly turned the lights off, picked up several packages needing to be mailed, and headed for the front door.

Juggling several boxes in one hand, she reached up to the small blue and white sign hanging from the back of the glass door.

She turned it from "Please Come In" to "Sorry We're Closed".

Jacqueline exited the shop, grabbed the doorknob with her free hand, and shut the locked door behind her.

As she turned around to head to her car, a light gust of wind blew a refreshing breeze from the lake. Jacqueline took a deep breath and looked up to the baby blue sky.

She closed her eyes and allowed the bright sunlight to warm her face.

"What a beautiful afternoon!"

The anticipation of getting out on the lake on such a beautiful day welled up inside her and caused her to accelerate her pace down the sidewalk.

Finally on the Road

One hundred and fifty miles to the south of the Crystal Lake, in the couples home town, Scott sat in his truck in front of a dry cleaners waiting for Darnisha to pick up her clean clothes. Slowly he glanced down at his bright orange Citizens diver's watch.

"Things always take longer than you figure," he muttered to himself as he rolled down the window.

This was the last of several errands they needed to get done before leaving.

Finally, Darnisha emerged from the storefront and smiled at him as she headed towards the truck.

She hung her freshly cleaned clothes on a hook on the inside above the back door.

Darnisha then opened the front door, and with a sigh of relief, climbed into the front seat and said,

"Let's get out of here!"

"You got it," Scott replied as he pulled their truck out of the parking lot and onto the main road.

After fifteen minutes and a dozen traffic lights, he finally navigated his Yukon onto the highway ramp.

He took a deep breath as he set the cruise control and settled back into his seat to get ready for the nearly three-hour ride.

It was an overcast day, but that didn't bother them at all. The couple were both excited to get out of town.

Scott reached over and clicked the iPod to his favorite jazz mix.

It didn't take long for Darnisha to start drifting to sleep.

Her inability to stay awake in a car was kind of a joke between the two of them. She fell asleep as Scott was driving on their first date.

Scott took it that she was so bored she couldn't stay awake. She assured him that she felt so relaxed and calm around him that she felt comfortable enough to fall asleep. Either way, he used it to tease her whenever driving in a car together.

Eventually, the couple had traveled beyond the outskirts of town and suburbs.

Now the landscape on either side of the highway was rolling green pastures outlined by groupings of mature maple and oak trees.

The farther the couple traveled north, the more the green pastures were overtaken by the trees.

Continuing north, the trees began to show off their fall colors. Red, yellow, burgundy, and orange became dominant over the green. Now and again green would retake its place because of the ever-increasing pine tree groves.

Soon the northbound highway began to take a gradual turn to the west.

The colorful trees ahead opened up to a beautiful valley below. The warm colors created an abstract work of art as the colors flowed back and forth across the hills.

Tracing the floor of the valley was a trout-filled river making its way towards Lake Michigan.

The breathtaking view warmed Scott's heart as soon as he saw it.

He felt really good about his life and had a confidence that things were going to be okay. He was happy to be married and really enjoying his new relationship with his wife.

It was a very rare moment in time for Scott where everything felt good.

It was peaceful.

He appreciated these times.

He'd had a rough road with relationships. He only dreamed that he would be married again; especially to a wonderful woman like Darnisha.

Scott's Rough Road

Scott grew up in church, a good kid.

He had a very strong sense of what was right and wrong from a young age.

He struggled his entire life with very low self-esteem and insecurity.

Unfortunately, his religious upbringing was quite twisted. It made him feel that God didn't love him enough to save him as it was explained to him.

Scott was taught that God would totally take away any desire and ability to sin if you were truly saved. Of course, that never happened.

He struggled for all of his preteen and teen years trying to obtain this magical salvation. Eventually, he gave up on it and acted the part to please his family while secretly starting to live a different life.

He "talked it" so well that he was asked to take over the college and career ministry at his church. He did it all while dating a stripper and with no experience of God, no relationship.

He desperately searched for something to find his own identity.

He soon found that he could make an identity in his family's furniture manufacturing business.

He started working for the company when he was 10 years old, mowing the lawn, and cleaning the factory.

Giving up all fun activities as a kid, he worked at the company after school and every summer.

He was a hard worker. His lack of self-worth pushed him even harder to make something of himself.

Soon he could operate every machine in the plant.

After high school he attended a Business University and earned himself the general manager position.

Scott had become a respected business professional... who found himself hating his career path. But the respect and image of a business executive was euphoric for him.

A wonderful mask he could hide behind.

From the outside he looked like he had it all together. Inside it was the exact opposite.

He still had no clue who he was.

He hung onto his career even tighter.

It was his identity but he still struggled.

He thought that being married would help him change his opinion of himself.

In his early twenties he found himself in a fiction-like, infatuation-based relationship. Being very naïve, he married young.

Having a beautiful, young, aggressive doctor pursue him so vigorously, made him feel good about himself.

He felt like he was living out a romance like he saw in the movies. He was doing all those things he saw that made what he perceived was love.

It was the only love Scott could have towards another person while hating himself.

He lived the fantasy to the fullest.

On the deck of a seventy-foot Hatteras motor yacht he chartered for a private cruise, he and his beautiful doctor watched the sunset, drank Dom Perignon, and fed each other strawberries.

He was living out everything he thought that a great relationship had.

The shy, immature twenty-two year old didn't have many relationships to draw from.

He knew he didn't want the relationship that his parents had. All he saw was arguing and bickering.

In less than a week of serious dating, Scott and his doctor began talking about marriage. Of course, it was on his speedboat five miles off shore while watching the sunset. To him it was all about the image, living what he thought was the dream.

The couple ended up eloping a month later in a romantic ceremony on Mackinaw Island.

Unfortunately, the whirlwind relationship quickly faced real world problems and dilemmas.

His dual lifestyle might have fooled his friends and family for a while but it couldn't work with a new wife around day and night.

He couldn't keep up the front anymore.

The reality that Scott didn't know who he was and was living a fantasy life came crashing down.

The couple began to fight a lot. In Scott's mind, the difficulties he was facing had to have come from this new person in his life. He never accounted for his warped ideas and dysfunctional life that drew him to the relationship in the first place. The couple ended up separated several times.

Finally, one day he came home from work and she had left, this time for good.

She said she couldn't take it anymore...and neither could he.

Scott hated the life he was living.

He wanted to live a life that was real, not one that was duplicated from some movie. He was tired of faking his way through a religious-looking life.

Scott wanted to find God.

It would all come to a head one Sunday morning. Merciful God answered Scott's heart cry.

It was a rough start for him that morning. With an emotional phone call from his soon to be ex-wife and a major mechanical failure with his truck, the enemy attempted to keep him away from church.

Demons attacked his mind with thoughts of depression. But God's call was on Scott's life.

This was a day of destiny; a day of new life.

He felt an urgency to get to church. He didn't know why. It just continued to lay heavy on his heart to push forward and not stay in a depressed funk.

Slowly he got out of bed and got ready for the long trip. It was a good forty-minute drive from his home northwest of town.

After his wife left left, Scott prayed, "God please help me find You."

Strangely enough God led him to an inner-city African American Pentecostal church.

It was very uncomfortable for him.

He was the only white person there.

Coming from a conservative background, he was not used to the lively services. He had never seen such excitement for the Lord before.

He had never been hugged so much in his life either. As strange as it all felt, God kept calling him back, week after week.

Little did Scott know that God's plan was not just for his salvation but training for his future training he would need for Pentecostal ministry. Training he would need to understand African American women.

He walked into church feeling depressed and defeated that fateful day.

The worship service was powerful.

The bishop was standing at the pulpit preparing to give his sermon.

Bishop was a very small man in stature but became a giant whenever he would sing or preach; a true man of God. This Sunday he preached on Jeremiah 1. He shared how "God formed us in our mother's womb and God has a master plan."

The words penetrated deep into Scott's heart. He hung on every one.

As he listened, his heart began to break. Tears began to flow down his cheeks.

On recollection of this moment in his life, he couldn't remember getting up and walking forward but that is exactly what he did.

He walked down the center isle of that old church. With tears streaming down, he looked up and saw Bishop smiling back at him with open arms.

Scott told him that he needed Christ in his life that day.

Bishop prayed with him.

The next thing he knew, he felt something like rushing waves flowing over his soul. His heart was overflowing with joy and thankfulness.

That morning Scott started his new life in Christ.

He would never be the same again.

The pain of the divorce did not go away. But he had someone to walk through it with him.

Unfortunately, he continued to use his career and money as a mask and crutch to lean on.

God did not like that. He wanted Scott to be who He made him to be. God wanted Scott to lean on Him and to know without a doubt that the new wife He had for him loved him for who he was.

So God began stripping the facade away from Scott's identity.

It was painful.

The country was in turmoil after the 9-11 tragedy and soon after the economy went bad.

Companies, when faced with falling profits, started cutting unnecessary items like new office furniture. Scott's family business was hit especially hard.

The business had just recovered from a major financial crisis and really needed a profitable year to solidify its financial standing. That didn't happen.

They were faced with two unfortunate options: one, lose the company and close the doors or, two, sell and at least save the jobs of the employees. Management opted for the latter. The company was sold for just enough to cover most of the major debts.

One of the partners of the group that purchased the company wanted Scott's position. Scott found himself without a job.

He was devastated.

His past and future, gone. His identity was gone.

He had to return the company Jaguar, the expense account, and the thing that hurt the worst, the business cards that said "Executive Vice President."

He was completely lost.

No one was hiring executives.

Before all of this went down, he had purchased a building near downtown. He was living on the second floor and had started building a Christian coffee house on the main floor. He wanted to use it as an outreach ministry.

After loosing his job, he decided to put all his time, effort, and remaining money into getting it open.

It was never meant to financially sustain itself. Scott had planned to support it with his executive income. But, he was so close to having it completed that he thought he might as well finish it. With God's grace and favor he did it.

He figured it would at least give him something to do and some income.

But, by the time he opened the coffeehouse, it had gobbled up all his savings. It brought in just enough money to cover the expenses. It barely gave him enough to live on. Thankfully, his family and friends donated time to help.

Scott found himself stripped of everything that gave him his identity.

His career, car, money, and future, all gone.

He felt completely vulnerable. There was nothing left to hide behind. For the first time in his life, he was not the one helping friends. Instead he had to be the one that friends helped out.

It was more than uncomfortable.

It was at this point in his life that he met the woman who changed his life.

Darnisha, unlike Scott, was very comfortable in her skin. She was a very lively person. She was fun to be around. She was usually the life of the party.

She found her passion and calling early in life and God blessed her in it.

She was a worship leader and very successful.

Not only was Darnisha an amazing worship leader, singer/songwriter, but she was also a musician, play-write, director, and actor. All this and a dynamic personality all packed into her nearly five foot two body.

In fact, the couple were pretty much opposites in everything. They where Mutt and Jeff even in their looks. Scott, a hulky six foot three Swedish American Indian, and Darnisha, a diminutive five foot African American.

But it was all right. It worked for them.

They filled in the gaps for each other. That is the purpose in marriage, to merge two souls together and become one that is more complete and well rounded.

The first time Scott had ever seen her was on a pair of 12 foot screens in the five thousand seat sanctuary where she lead worship every Sunday.

Scott was still struggling with a bad attitude with God. He was frustrated that God called him away from his spiritual birthplace, the inner-city church, to a suburban predominately white church.

Scott had no idea that this move would change his life forever, for the better. He had no idea that he would meet his other half, his soul mate, his wife. Like so many times in life, you find things in the last place you would think to look.

Darnisha was a minister of music at one of the largest churches in Western Michigan.

Scott thought she was attractive.

As he listened to her each Sunday he realize that there was something more to her singing than just a good voice. She was first and foremost a worshiper who happened to sing.

He began to look forward to hearing and seeing her each Sunday.

The music was not as dynamic as what he had grown accustomed to at his prior church.

The level of worship though blew his former experience away.

Scott decided to do some research on her. He typed her name into the Internet.

He found out that she traveled with a famous speaker who was a Vietnam vet, with an amazing testimony of surviving a grenade blast.

He found out she was a part of the music department at a local University. She also directed a 150-voice gospel choir there and had a CD.

"This girl really has it together. If I ever got married again, it would be to someone like her," was his conclusion.

Months later, Scott was riding home from church with friends.

They announced to him that they had to make a stop at a new acquaintance's birthday party. Scott immediately felt uneasy. He was not the kind of person that drops in on people, especially ones he didn't know.

He and his friends pulled up to a very nice home and rang the doorbell.

The door opened and to Scott's utter shock, stood Darnisha. It was her birthday.

All the blood rushed to his head and a nervous knot instantly formed in his stomach.

He could tell that she wasn't used to people she didn't know showing up at her home.

Scott's friends introduced him to her and she invited them all in.

Her family and friends were eating in between uproars of laughter.

This was not a stiff starchy group of people.

They all made Scott feel right at home and soon the knot in his stomach began to untie.

Several weeks later, the coffeehouse opened for business.

Now Scott was working 14-hour days trying to get a new business afloat. Not much time for any kind of a social life.

One day, to his surprise, Darnisha walked into the coffeehouse.

She loved his Italian sodas and just had to have one.

He knew his drinks were good, but not good enough for anyone to drive to the opposite end of town for one. She was interested. He played it real cool though.

She stayed and they talked for a while. Both could feel connections being made.

Over the next few months, she kept coming in for an Italian soda, each time staying longer. They really enjoyed talking.

By now, it was around the holiday time. One of Darnisha's friends became a regular at the coffeehouse.

One day after he finished his triple cappuccino, he came up to the counter and asked Scott " Would you host a New Year's party here at your coffeehouse for our small group?"

Scott had no idea that it was Darnisha that put her friend up to it.

"That would be great. Let's do it!"

A few days later, Scott got a call from Darnisha asking if he needed any help setting up for the party. He encouraged her to come over the night of the party a little early.

She was very excited to have some alone time with him and showed up three hours early.

He was surprised but glad she came.

Being older and a bit wiser, he decided to be straightforward with her about his difficult past.

She was taken aback. She didn't realize he was divorced and had a much more colorful past than she.

She wasn't sure how she felt about it. But she still was interested in knowing him more.

The party was a success. It rolled on until 4:00 am in the morning.

The next evening, Scott was excited to get a call from Darnisha inviting him over to hang out with some friends. The couple enjoyed each other's company more and more. The following week they hung out with her friends every day.

They really were feeling comfortable around each other. She turned into quite a flirt.

He decided to ask her out on an official date.

He worked up some courage and called her.

To his utter surprise she said, "No.".

She said she had prayed about it already and that she couldn't date him.

He was crushed.

He was perplexed that he could have misread her signals.

With that, he assumed the door was closed. But, he was not able to get her out of his thoughts and heart. So, he called another girl and went out that weekend. It didn't help.

Sunday he tried to play it off to her as if it were no big deal.

It was, for both of them.

Darnisha had a restless night's sleep. If she wasn't supposed to date him why did she have such intense feelings for him? She went to prayer.

"Why, Lord, do I have these feeling if I cannot be with him?"

The Lord's answer was waiting their for her to ask the question. "I didn't say you cannot be with him. I said you cannot 'date' him. With this relationship you cannot come nonchalantly. This man has been through too much. This has to be a commitment towards a potential future together."

Relieved, she responded, "All right, Lord. I am serious. I want this. I feel like a fool. He is going to think I am a flake." "Don't worry, my Daughter. I will take care of his heart. Just be humble."

God dispatched Enoch to prepare Scott's heart for Darnisha's revelation.

That night, Scott felt peace and slept soundly.

Monday, he received a call from her closest friend. She told him that Darnisha really wanted to date him. She felt embarrassed that she turned him down.

He was confused. But, told her friend that he was willing to talk. Minutes later, Darnisha called and asked if she could come down to his coffeehouse.

He said, "Sure." Ten minutes later, she walked meekly into the restaurant.

"Hey! Ah, can we talk in private?" she asked sheepishly.

"Sure. Let's go upstairs."

The couple sat down in Scott's living room. Both were very uncomfortable.

She slowing began to explain her response to his invitation.

"After I told you 'no' I couldn't shake the feelings I was having. So, I had to pray again and ask for clarity. That's when God explained what I had misunderstood. I don't mean to sound strange, but I feel like He said that I may not approach this as I have other relationships lately. He won't allow me to casually date you. I'm not saying we're suppose to get married or anything, but this has to be more serious than passive."

He could tell as they sat there that this was difficult for her. She looked nervous and awkward.

"So," she continued, "If you are interested in seriously dating, we can talk more. If you are not , then I can go."

Scott looked over and smiled at her. "Let's keep talking." She smiled back at him with relief and joy.

The couple set up an official date up for later that evening.

Their first kiss was 3 months after that date. They were married a year and a half later.

Crystal Lake

After traveling on a westerly heading, Scott turned his SUV onto M27, a little two-lane highway heading north, cut through a seeming endless forest of ancient trees.

He felt his heart starting to beat faster.

A flutter grew in his stomach.

They would soon be getting the first view of the lake.

Scott noticed a pocket of clear blue sky amongst the dense cloud-covered area in the distant northwest. In fact, it was a divine clearing created around the area of Crystal Lake where the couple was headed.

As Scott and Darnisha got closer to their destination, she awoke from her nap and grabbed his hand.

"Can we make an agreement not to argue on this trip north?" she asked softly.

The couple had a bit of a history of arguments when they traveled north.

Scott didn't know if it was just that they would allow things to surface as they became more relaxed or if it was resurfacing feelings from past trips with his ex-wife. Deep down he felt that it was more likely the latter of the two.

He felt terrible about it.

"Baby, I promise we won't have an argument on this trip."

She smiled and said, "I love you." He echoed back.

He truly did love Darnisha with all his heart. He'd had a rocky road, to say the least, with relationships and marriage. He had been divorced for about seven years before he met her and had pretty much given up on the whole marriage concept.

He had dated after his divorce, but felt that he was no longer able to love, truly love another woman the way he thought he should. Then he met Darnisha and that thought was soon torn from his mind and heart forever.

The road crested the top of a small hill and just on the other side, a picturesque view of Crystal Lake and the quaint shore village of Beulah.

The overcast sky with heavy gray clouds had given way to amazingly brilliant blue over the lake and surrounding area.

The adjacent hills were bursting with warm fall colors as they sloped down to the shores of the lake.

The couple turned off the main road and onto a side road heading around the northwest part of the lake.

Scott's excitement grew.

Darnisha's grew as well but mainly from anxiety and nervousness over the dive.

Pretty normal feelings for someone who has not dove recently.

The small two-lane road wound tightly around the lake, following its contour perfectly.

Several spots of the road came to within a few feet of the water's edge.

After seeing this lake for the first time one did not have to figure out how it got its name. The crystal blue water sparkled brilliantly as it reflected the sunrays streaming down from a now clear blue sky.

An untamed smile grew on Scott's face; one of his favorite places, doing his favorite activity, with his favorite person.

Still, after years of searching, Scott had not found his purpose in life.

People pleasing and following other people's advice had buried his passion so deep, that the spark in his heart seemed too dim to find. But, scuba diving was that one ember of hope.

He was encouraged to discover it by friends of the rarest kind, friends who wanted only the best for him.

After hearing Scott constantly talk about the ocean and sea life they persuaded him to take scuba lessons. They not only talked him into it, but put their love for him into action and took the classes with him.

As much as Scott loved the idea of the water, he had a great fear of it that started at a very young age. Oddly enough, through the fear, there was something that beckoned him to the water like a moth to a flame. His desire for it burned inside him. He had not experienced that with anything in his life.

Scott was gripped with fear throughout the in-water sessions in class. But, perseverance and a heart longing to break out, pushed him to complete the course and swung a door open to his future.

He discovered that he adored it.

It fed his soul.

Once he conquered the fear, he experienced something more freeing, uplifting, and magical than he ever had before. Underwater he saw wonders of God's creation that were beyond words. He could fly over the splendor as his soul listened to nature sing praises to its Creator.

It became a spiritual experience that connected him to God. It was a place of peace. The cares of the world could not follow him as he dropped below the surface of the waves.

With each dive, he would experience a new baptism, a renewing of his spirit; a time where he and his Savior enjoyed a walk together through the submerged Eden.

The entrance for the location on the lake that Scott had made his official dive spot was tricky to find.

Spotting the narrow dirt driveway among the many trees and beautiful vacation homes was nearly impossible and easy to miss altogether.

Scott dove from this spot every time he visited Crystal Lake. He was extremely familiar with how the lake was laid out from this point.

Most of the time, he dove by himself. He knew it sounded unsafe, but he had taken many advanced diving classes, as well as studied solo diving.

So, he was actually more comfortable diving alone than with someone. It was easier for him to calculate the potential risks and accept them for himself, but he was not comfortable doing so for someone else.

As Darnisha grew more interested in the sport and became a certified diver, Scott became more conservative in where and how he would dive. Sometimes, he thought that it might be fun to dive from a different point. But, the idea of a new dive spot with a foreign terrain was out of the question today. He wanted to be completely comfortable and confident with Darnisha on this dive.

As he finalized the decision in his mind, he saw the small dirt road he was searching for just as he began to pass it. With an abrupt stop and swerve into a driveway, he quickly corrected his error.

The narrow grassy area led back from the road to a short rocky slope into the lake.

He swung the truck around and backed up to the edge of the slope and parked about ten feet from the water's edge.

They stepped out of the SUV into the warm sunlight.

Scott took a deep breath of the wonderfully refreshing air.

"This is a beautiful day and a great idea," he thought to himself.

Darnisha opened the back of the truck and began to get her gear ready.

Scott jumped back into the truck and turned the key and clicked on the iPod. He advanced it to one of their favorite romantic mixes.

Darnisha looked up at him with a sexy glance. He got out of the truck and walked back to where she was, put his arms around her and kissed her.

She whispered, "Why don't we get in the back of the truck for a little while?" ending the question with a light groan.

Scott responded, "Oh, that sounds very nice!"

It is amazing what a look and sexy sound can trigger in a man. A drive so deep that it instantly incapacitates him and makes him forget his own name.

For a brief moment, Scott forgot where he was and what they were planning to do.

As he was able to break the hypnotizing look in Darnisha's eyes, he caught a glimpse of the sun and its movement towards the west. It was getting late.

If they climbed into the back of the truck, they would not be climbing back out until long after the sun had gone.

He responded softly, "I would love to, Baby, but if we don't get our dive in now, we won't get it in at all."

"O.K... you're right, Honey," she said with a little disappointment in her voice.

"We can address that as soon as the dive is done," he reassured her.

"All right then; let's get this thing over with," she quickly stated.

They laughed.

He smacked her on the rear and they began to get their gear set up

Running Late for Fishing

Jacqueline, driving towards home, glanced down at the digital clock on the dash of her car. "Wow, where did the day go?" she said out loud.

Her few errands turned into a full day's worth of work. Normally, situations like this put her into a frustrated mood. Any other day, she would have called off the fishing trip with no hesitation and been angry the rest of the evening.

For some reason she felt a peculiar peace about the lateness of the day. In fact, going later just felt right.

Her peace of mind was no coincidence.

Jacqueline guardian, Vohumanah, had been encouraging her to keep working until the ordained time and gave her joy through it.

She turned onto her road just a few blocks from the main street of the coastal village.

She pulled into her driveway alongside her quaint white house. The scene depicted exactly what one's imagination drums up when envisioning a small town neighborhood.

Half way to the front door, she was greeted by the sound of her German Shepherd excitable barking "Hello." She opened the door and out flew Trixie jumping on and licking her as if they had been apart for weeks.

"Trixie, get down. Calm down, girl."

Jacqueline pleaded with no avail as she pushed her way inside the house and up the stairs to change her clothes for fishing.

As she was changing, Trixie ran to the front window and started barking again with mad excitement. Moments later, Jacqueline heard the door and the voice of her husband Patrick trying to get Trixie to make room for him to enter.

"Trixie! Down, Trixie! Yah, I missed you, too. Back up; get away from the door."

Trixie's ears went down, her tail began to wag more fiercely, and her tongue started to lick the air in anticipation of licking her master's face.

With a hard push from his shoulder, the door opened enough for Trixie to slide through. Immediately she jumped up on Patrick almost face to face and began her ritual licking like a kid with her first lollipop.

"Jackie, are you still here?" Patrick shouted as he pushed Trixie aside.

"Yeah, I am here!" Jacqueline shouted in return.

"I thought you were going fishing?" Patrick inquired looking up the stairs. Jacqueline emerged from their bedroom pulling her shirt down over her shorts.

"I still am going fishing," she said.

"I thought you were going early this afternoon?" Patrick questioned as she made her way down the steps.

"I was", Jacqueline replied, "I just got carried away with my errands and the day was gone." "And you are still talking and not growling at me?! Are you all right? Usually you turn into a raging monster when your plans don't work out." Patrick jokingly ribbed Jacqueline and prepared to get smacked back.

Jacqueline replied back in a confused tone, "I know!? It just feels okay today."

Patrick chuckled and smiled as Jacqueline walked by him into the kitchen.

"Wow, miracles never cease!"

"Ha, Ha, very funny." Jacqueline sarcastically responded. "Do you want to come with us?"

A moment of silence passed as Patrick stared out the window. Slowly, with a bit of hesitation in his voice he replied, "Sure, I'll go with you."

Jacqueline was totally taken by surprise with his answer. She always asks Patrick to join the girls' fishing trip knowing that she would undoubtedly hear a "No Way!" response from Patrick's mouth.

"Cool! Go get ready; I'll get the gear in the car. Let's get going!" Jacqueline directed as she threw some sodas and snacks in a cooler and headed for the garage.

"I'll call Peggy and let her know we are on our way. Make sure to feed Trixie before you come out," were the last words Patrick could make out as Jacqueline exited the house through the screen door at the back of the kitchen.

He rushed upstairs to change his clothes. In a flash, he was back down the stairs just as he heard the horn from Jacqueline's car.

The laid back Patrick smiled and shook his head as he headed into the kitchen and over to the pantry to get dog food with Trixie hot on his heels.

He filled the bowl, returned the enormous bag to the pantry, and headed out the back door. As he shut and locked the door, he heard an extended horn blow, this time followed by a "Come on!" from his now impatient wife.

Patrick shook his head again as he turned towards the car and responded with a "Yeah, yeah, yeah."

Jacqueline, in the running car, had her arm out the window waving Patrick to get in. Patrick headed towards the car with his head down, a big grin on his face and a hand up waving back at Jacqueline.

As he got in the car, he announced, "What are we waiting for? Let's get going." Jacqueline let out a laughing huff as she pulled out of the driveway and made her way to the boat docks less than five minutes from their house.

Gearing Up

Scott was sorting through all his gear in his Yukon.

He had learned from his extensive training and experience that it was always better to have too much equipment than not have what you needed.

As he glanced over the gear, Enoch, Scott's guardian, planted a thought in his mind. "Bring two dive flags." As he held both flags in his hands, he said to himself,

"What am I going to do with two of these?"

There was no one on the lake, so they didn't have to worry about being extra careful to be seen by boaters.

In that moment, Enoch whispered to Scott, "Put one stationary flag in at your entry point and tow the other one along with you."

"That makes sense," Scott thought. He had never even thought of doing this before, but it seemed like something he should do today.

By now, Darnisha was all geared up and standing knee deep in the lake.

Scott shut the truck and hid the keys in the Reese hitch at the rear of the truck.

Skillfully and stealthfully the Buffeter Demon made its way into the physical realm.

The Buffeter Demons were praised for their ability to find small obscure items and opportunities to launch small unassuming attacks against the Children of God. Attacks that would "buffet" the soul in such a crafty way that it would seem like an event of human forgetfulness or simple error. They quickly assessed the situation and area as the couple waded out into the water with their equipment. Immediately, the demons attention went to the couple's equipment as they tied it all to their BC's and floated it alongside them in the water.

As Darnisha dropped her gear in the water the demon saw the opportunity he was looking for, one that would get beyond her husband's watchful eye.

The coupling connecting the BC to the airline was not connected yet.

With glee, the demon swam over and directed one grain of sand to lodge its way into the coupling between the outer wall and the ball bearing.

"There, that's all we need," it sneered then slithered into the lakes dark depths to wait the legion soon to come.

It was a long walk to get to the ledge where they could start their dive.

The lake was only four feet deep for a good two hundred and fifty yards.

After that, there was a drop off that abruptly descended forty-five feet then gradually descended again to the maximum depth of the lake, one hundred and forty feet.

Scott and Darnisha continued slowly to the first ledge.

This was always one of his favorite times in a dive, the moments right before submersion. The world always seemed more vibrant and exciting.

Little did he know that this would be the most eventful dive of his life.

Scott turned and smiled at his wife who was a half dozen yards behind. He put on the remaining equipment that he had been floating.

He checked his gear by purging the primary and secondary regulators and took a big breath out of each. With great excitement, he lowered his black silicon mask onto his face and released the air from his buoyancy control vest, "BC" for short. He sank to the shallow bottom.

Now face down on the floor of the lake, Scott felt confident that he had plenty of weight on. He left several pounds off to help compensate for the oversized tank that he rented for the dive that day.

Glancing up from the bottom, he could see beyond the edge of the drop off into the deep blue water.

Returning to the surface, he saw Darnisha standing beside him checking her gear once more. He asked with a smile and a touch of impatience, "Are you ready?" She nodded her head "yes" as she pulled her mask over her face.

He did a "360" noting how beautiful the lake and surrounding landscape was. He took a deep breath of the fresh air, put his regulator in his mouth and with her right beside him, they headed down the sloped bottom of the lake.

Act II

The Production Begins

At the lake, Azariel who ruled over the winds, began preparing for the deathgate to appear. Nature was already sensing that something supernatural was about to take place and began to react to the coming event.

Azariel took authority over the winds and clouds and held them at bay around the lake.

The scene was set…

The cast was assembled…

It was time for the curtain to rise on the master playwright's production.

God Almighty would conduct this supernatural performance, the deathgate, His plan.

As God raised His baton to start the heavenly orchestra, all of creation inhaled in anticipation. The baton fell, the composition began. It was beautiful and complete. It was a song of courage, victory, and grace. As the Master's masterpiece faded to completion, another composition could be heard echoing from afar. It was distinctively different.

It was strong, intentional, and aggressive. Horns could be heard getting louder and louder. It was a call to arms, a battle cry.

The turbulence in the spiritual realm was so great that it sent the area around the lake into chaos. Even the animals sensed that something powerful was happening and began to scatter in confusion.

 The power of the perfection of God created great tension in the fallen realm.

The churning in the spirit realm caused a massive opening through the overlying ceiling of clouds covered that covered the area. From miles away an immense oval hole through the clouds revealing the crystal blue sky could be seen.

Through the blue sky, the hosts of heaven came rushing in like a mighty wind and encircled the area armed and ready for battle.

Then from the power that created the endless expanse of stars, planets, and infinite universes, the deathgate exploded into its time as the birth of a star in heaven.

All the realms of heaven and hell trembled with great fury. Yet this incredible event and appearance of the deathgate created the opposite effect on the physical realm.

Confused and perplexed, all of nature went deadly still. The winds ceased, the creatures of earth fled in fear their senses heightened with impending danger.

 The disturbance stole the songs from nearby birds of the air.

The fish retreated to the dark deepest depths of the lake. The unnatural sound of complete silence fell across the lake.

As nature began to recover from the shock and disturbance, it began to react violently to the intrusion. The winds and waves began to crash everywhere on the lake except an area circling the deathgate.

Within the circle, the sky above remained crystal blue and the waters as smooth as glass. No creature on earth crossed into the circle.

The only physical beings near the deathgate were the couple, Scott and Darnisha.

The appearance of the deathgate was awe-inspiring even for the immortals.

It was enormous and appeared to be crafted out of stones that were ancient before time began. The enormity surpassed the boundaries of the realm of the gateways down into the physical realm and into the very foundations of the earth.

Then, in the distance, a horrifying screech echoed through heaven. It was the sound of the rushing wind being beaten methodically. Accompanying the sound was a smell of sulfur and old death. It was squadrons of demons that were flying from the nether regions of darkness.

Out of the belly of darkness came demons, tormentors, and creatures of evil that mortal minds could not begin to grasp.

Out front of the squadron was Dezro proudly leading them into battle.

The creatures flew around the deathgate furling insults and blasphemy, mocking its purpose.

Several demons, in utter disrespect, landed on the top of the deathgate and began sodomizing each other; others defecated on it.

Other demons began attaching themselves like viny weeds clinging to the ancient stones of the gate. They clawed and bit furiously at the structure at its foundation to corrupt and weaken and distort its purpose.

As they clung to the stones, they stretched out to those who pass through to grab and distract as they hiss words of doubt and fear, words of corruption and destruction.

So rare a scene is this.

Prophets of old once wrote if humans could see what was happening in their midst in the spiritual realm their soul would immediately flee from their bodies for their physical eyes could not bare the sight.

Then a trumpet blast like an aftershock of an explosion or massive earthquake rang across the endless space.

It was a sound heard by the immortals throughout the endless ages of eternity. A sound that sent shivers to the core of the rancid diseased hearts of the demon army.

The sound created a spark deep within the Angelic beings of heaven and ignited into a flame of glorious victory. The all-consuming flame no longer containable by the hosts, exploded out of them in the form of a battle cry.

With that, the hosts of heaven began to engage the demons of hell as they attempted to distract the couple and distort the purpose of the gateway.

The battle to assist the Taylors' through the deathgate had begun.

Centurions Release Nature

As Scott and Darnisha dipped below the surface of the water only air bubbles were left to indicate their entry.

Just then Jesus called to Azariel, the centurion of the winds.

"Unleash the winds across the lake; Sachiel, centurion of the waters, allow the waters to be turned and foam. But, cup your hands around the portion where my children are. Keep this area calm."

Obediently, Azariel released the winds. With the wave of his hand the winds blew heavy across the large lake.

Then Sachiel dragged his fingers through the water causing waves to leap up and foam.

Several angles from the centurion squadron hovered over the diving area to form a circle barrier at the surface of the water. This circle provided a shield that deflected the winds. Azariel calmed the waters in that area to make it quite different from the others.

Two demons skillfully maneuvered passed the centurions and shot like rockets into the water. They began to stir the sands beneath the crystal clear waters. They stirred the sands and silt so violently that the vibrant aquamarine became a foggy greenish brown.

Scott turned to drift down backwards over the ledge so that he could look up at Darnisha. She checked her gear and followed trustingly. Looking to him for constant support and comfort.

He was really paying attention to her body language to be sure that she felt comfortable and was not having any problems getting down.

On their previous dive at California's Lake Tahoe, she had a little difficulty with equalizing her ears. At the time, Scott racked it up to the altitude since Lake Tahoe is in the mountains and a mile above sea level. That was her first altitude dive and technical dive with formulas to calculate for the pressure differences.

With that experience and since the first ten feet in diving is the highest-pressure change to the body, they stopped for a moment to make sure she could equalize fully before continuing.

Scott lifted his hand and formed a circle with his thumb and pointer finger, the universal dive sign to ask if your dive buddy is "OK." She returned the sign. Everything was fine. She was feeling good and so was he.

He turned and continued down, hovering two feet off the sandy bottom. She followed suit just above him to the left where she swam when they dove together.

Glancing up, he could see her. It reminded him of the first time they dove together at Crystal Lake.

She was still in scuba training and was practicing by using his secondary regulator. She wore no equipment beside her mask and just held onto his back.

Now, at this dive, Darnisha was no beginner.

She was decked out in all the best scuba equipment money could buy. Darnisha had several dives under her belt not only in California, but also in the Florida Keys. While diving the keys she took advanced training so that she could dive shipwrecks.

After her first wreck dive, the Dwaine, an awesome upright wreck sitting in 130 feet she was hooked.

She became bored with reef dives.

That is, until one reef dive where they came across two seven foot nurse sharks. Scott eyed the sharks first tucked under a ledge on a coral reef. He had a great fascination with them and wanted to do a shark dive.

Darnisha was emphatically against it. So, naturally, he didn't point them out to her.

But she spotted them.

He looked at her and gave her the OK sign.

To his surprise, she returned it that time. So, he moved in for a closer look. Now less than 3 feet from them, he reached out to touch one of them and they swam away in the opposite direction.

For Scott, it was an exhilarating moment.

He wasn't sure how Darnisha felt about it.

They finished the dive soon after and headed back.

Darnisha was in the boat first.

From the moment she got her regulator out of her mouth, she couldn't stop talking about the sharks she had seen.

By the time Scott sat down and got his gear off, she had decided that she was ready to go on a shark dive now, but Scott refused.

He would consider doing things that he would not want her to do and shark diving was one of them.

He could handle the idea of being bitten, but couldn't take it if she were.

Today, there were no sharks in the cold Northern Michigan lake, but he was nonetheless just as cautious with his precious bride.

The Other Side of the Lake

Patrick and Jacqueline arrived at the small dock where they kept their boat. The little white run-about was perfect for any activity you would want to do on the water.

As Patrick jumped out of the car, he noticed the unusual weather. Jacqueline stepped out and felt the strong east wind. As she walked towards the boat, she looked out over the lake and noticed how choppy it had become.

"Wow, where did this come from?" she asked Patrick.

"Yah, looks a little rough. You still want to go out?"

"Heck, yes! I am going fishing today!"

"Ok, I was just asking," Patrick replied sheepishly as he continued to remove the boat cover.

Just then a "beep, beep" came from the parking lot where Peggy was pulling up next to Jacqueline's car.

Jacqueline waved with a smile.

Peggy stepped out of her car and popped her trunk to grab her pole and a small tackle box. She walked towards the dock and took a deep breath.

"What a beautiful day to have the lake to ourselves!"

Just then Jacqueline noticed that there wasn't anyone else around.

"Wow, it's strange that no one is out today, huh. Great! More fish for us," she laughed.

As Peggy walked down the dock alongside the boat, she said,

"Pat is coming with us? To what do we owe this rare privilege?"

 Patrick smiled at Peggy as he offered his hand to help her into the boat.

"Hey, I like fishing once in awhile."

"Great! We need someone to bate the hooks for us," Peggy joked as she stepped into the boat with a wobble.

They were taking their time but Jacqueline felt an urgency to get going.

"I am feeling anxious. Let's get rollin'." "You got it!"

Finally on their way, Patrick drove the boat out to their normal spot. The heavy wind and waves made it too difficult to do any fishing here.

"Hey, let's see how it is on the other side of the lake." Jacqueline and Peggy both looked at Patrick with stunned expressions.

"Pat, you want to drive all the way to the other side of the lake to see if the weather is better? You hate going to that side!," said Jacqueline.

"Yeah, Yeah, I know but I just got a feeling we are going to find some great catches over there. I can't explain it. A gut feeling I guess"

So Patrick turned into the wind and started across the now choppy lake. The trio braced themselves for the long ride. As they pounded along from wave to wave Jacqueline looked up at the sky.

"Wow, I have not seen a sky like that over the lake. Check out the swirling clouds, and look at how the sunlight is shooting through like laser beams. I wish I'd brought my camera."

Things Were Not Right

As Darnisha and Scott went deeper, they noticed that the water had an eerie brown haze to it. He glanced back at her as she swam along his left side.

Even though they were very close, it was hard to see each other clearly.

The water was extremely cloudy. This was something Scott had never experienced diving this location.

The lake boasts clear blue water, with fifty to seventy five feet of visibility. Today was eight feet at best.

Scott was disappointed.

One of the main reasons for coming to Crystal Lake was the incredible visibility.

Still, they headed down the drop off until they came to the first semi-flat ledge.

On this ledge, short grassy patches grew creating a small camouflaged forest for crawfish. Scott enjoyed catching them for his Cajun crawfish jambalaya.

Darnisha could not stand them. They were like giant ugly sea monsters even though they were two inches in length at best. Still, she stayed as far from them as she could.

This time, he left the crawfish alone and just glided over them.

The couple continued to swim west along the drop off running parallel to the shoreline. Another reason that this lake was a great dive spot was that whenever you were done with your dive, you simply turned around and followed the drop off back.

After a lengthy swim, Scott and Darnisha reached an area in which the lay of the lake seemed to change abruptly. There was a break in the drop off. They kept swimming along in what they thought was westerly direction, in order to find the drop off line again.

Scott started to feel uneasy.

Something didn't feel right this time.

Things didn't seem familiar.

He decided to turn around and head back. Darnisha was close behind. As they swam, he realized that somehow they had lost the ledge again.

He stopped and knelt on the bottom trying to get his bearing. He turned to Darnisha to use the compass on her gear.

As she knelt beside him, he noticed a very small but steady stream of bubbles coming from her gear. Looking closer, he found that it was coming from the coupler that attached an airline to her BC. This line powered the inflator for the BC with a push of a button, rather than having to inflate it manually.

Thinking that it wasn't attached properly, he grabbed hold of the coupler and wiggled it.

The stream didn't stop.

He pulled hard on the coupler. It detached from its place.

He attempted to reattach it but it would not go down around the male end of the inflator, so he left the hose alone.

Darnisha still had the manual inflator. As an advanced diver, she was trained extensively to manage for just such an occasion.

Scott's attention went to the compass.

He held it straight in front of him and waited for it to stop moving.

Three of the demons continued stirring up the water. One conjured up a false magnetic field to interfere with the compass reading.

"This should help create some confusion for them," the demon chuckled to the other two.

Slowly the compass stopped.

Scott took a heading of what he thought was north, back towards the drop off. They started swimming with their new heading.

After a short distance, Scott noticed that it was getting darker and the visibility was getting worse.

They couldn't see anything except the sandy bottom two feet below them.

His uneasiness began to increase.

All of a sudden, a chill hit his entire body.

It was the thermal cline. A thermal cline is a line in the water where heavier cold water meets the lighter warmer water. It is a very unique sensation because it is not gradual. One second you are in 65 degree water, the next you are in 45.

"This is not right. We should be getting to shallower water or at least staying at the same depth. We should not be going deeper," he thought.

He stopped abruptly.

He knelt on the bottom again and turned to Darnisha to take another reading on the compass. By this time, she was getting nervous. Since she had never been a strong swimmer or even much of a water sports kind of girl, she always relied on Scott to be the confident one underwater.

Seeing him question, made her anxiety begin to surface.

Scott took another reading on the compass.

Based on past experience, he thought they were going in the right direction.

"How could we have gotten so turned around?" Scott thought.

Normally, he had an amazing sense of direction, especially in a familiar diving situation. Scott, still kneeling on the bottom, stared at the compass. He closed his eyes and tried to rationalize how this could have happened.

He couldn't make sense of it.

Now they were in nearly seventy feet of dark murky water.

At that moment, he made a decision that he would regret for the rest of his life.

Using hand signals, he motioned for Darnisha to follow the flag rope up to the surface and get a bearing on where they were in relation to their entry point. He also gestured for her to try to attach her hose to her BC again.

He thought that the ascent to the surface would be easier using the rope as a point of reference rather than doing a blind ascent. It is very crucial for a diver to control his ascent to the surface. A maximum ascent rate is only about a foot per second. Trying to do this without any point of reference and low visibility, it is very challenging, especially in an anxious situation; so, Scott stayed on the bottom of the lake and secured the ascension rope for his bride.

Three demons plunged into the water towards Scott.

A water centurion saw them. He clenched his sword in his enormous hand and started towards them. The heavenly commander stopped the centurion.

"Let them be. The Lord has a purpose for them."

Darnisha started up to the surface.

Scott watched her become a dark shadow and disappear into the brown cloudy water. He looked down at his dive computer to check his remaining air.

The demons swirled around Scott, darting back and forth allowing their shadows to be visible to his physical eye. They laughed with glee as they saw his concern grow, watching the dark shadows pass around him. "This will plant a perfect seed of fear in his mind!" they scoffed.

While Scott was looking down at his dive computer, he thought he saw something out of the corner of his eye.

It was a dark mass moving rapidly.

He turned his head quickly to see what the thing was, but there was nothing. Then again on the opposite side, he saw it again.

Still he couldn't make out what seemed to be lurking around him.

He checked his dive computer again to make sure his levels were all right.

Everything was fine.

He stared at the bottom, the only true reference point he had.

As he looked up again, the dark mass darted across in front of him in the water.

His anxiety was building.

Time seemed to creep by.

He started wondering why Darnisha wasn't coming back down.

After waiting for what seemed an eternity, yet it was only five minutes, he decided to abort the dive and ascend to the surface. He was really feeling uncomfortable being separated this long.

By this time, the dark masses had created a fear in him that crept into his spirit.

They Began to Worship

The bubbly Chinese woman invited her friends into her humble apartment.

The guests entered and took seats in her small room that served as a sitting, living, and dining room. They continued catching up with the activities of the week since they last met. "How's your family?," "Work?," "Has God brought any new people into your life this week?", were the topics of discussion.

As the conversation slowed down, the woman invited her guests to pray.

All of them lowered themselves to their knees and bowed their heads in sincere reverence. It was as if someone of royalty had just entered the room… and in fact He had. The presence of the Holy Spirit was overwhelming.

"My merciful Savior and Lord, thank you for sending your son Jesus to die for my sins and giving us eternal life. Thank you for your gift of the Holy Spirit that lives in our hearts giving guidance and wisdom. Thank you for the freedom of worship and we ask you now, Father, that you would come and be pleased with our praises to you. We praise you, Almighty God, for this wonderful new life you have given us. With our last breath, we will praise your name for what you have done for us, in the name of our Savior, Jesus Christ."

Just then, the small group began to worship. The sound of prayers, praises, and songs filled the room.

As they were caught up in praise and worship to God, the woman thought she heard an unusual thump.

She stopped her praising and listened more closely.

There it was again, several bumps.

It was coming from the direction of her front door.

Wondering what it could be, she walked towards it to find out. "I don't think we were being too loud that we are disturbing my neighbors," she thought. As she started to turn the knob, it flung open with a loud crash.

The door swung wide and fast sending doorjamb splinters flying into the air and hitting her as it opened.

The force of the impact hurled her small body hard into the wall and onto the small table, shattering it and the lamp that rested on it. As she fell to the floor, her head hit the edge of the table causing her neck to twist and jerk. Her body collapsed to the ground like a rag doll. She lay motionless on the broken pieces.

Through the now open door rushed several uniformed and heavily armed soldiers. They shouted orders and began to manhandle the stunned small group, pushing them to the ground face first.

One of the ladies twisted till she broke free from her captor and ran to the woman on the floor. She called out her name frantically… no response.

She placed her hand on her shoulder and began to shake her gently. As she shook her, the humble waitress' body rolled towards her and slowly onto her back. Her eyes were wide open and lifeless. A thin stream of blood ran out of her nose and the corner of her mouth...she was gone.

Darnisha's Ascent

As Darnisha ascended, she noticed that Scott was quickly out of view… too quickly.

She saw him for less than ten feet; then her only reference to his presence was the stable rope she was ascending on.

She made her safety stop at ten feet from the surface for three minutes. No problem. After three minutes she continued slowly to the surface.

Dezro followed her and began to whisper confusing ideas to her. She was already feeling anxious. Now this.

"Ok, I know what to do…I think. Just do what you're supposed to do. Fix the coupler. No problem, Darnisha, " she thought to herself.

As she broke the surface, she made her first mistake. Instead of manually inflating her BC, she tried to fix the coupler attaching the air hose. All the while kicking and treading to stay on the surface, resisting the pull of the weight attached to her gear.

With demons still causing confusion, she struggled with the coupler. It would not connect.

"Oh, God, I can't get it! Lord, please help me get this!" Out loud she prayed. She had not realized how fatigued she was getting as she struggled to keep her head above water. Even though she was trained for such an emergency, she relied on her equipment to work, maybe too much. Without the assistance of her inflated BC, she became winded.

"Oh, Lord. I need my husband. God, help me." She was nervous and winded, but still felt she could resolve this problem but couldn't think of how at the moment. This glimmer of confidence quickly faded.

Dezro taunted Darnisha, filling her mind with confusion. Israfel tried to keep Dezro at bay, but other demons swooped in to distract her. So Dezro continued his attacks on Darnisha's thoughts.

With the little breath she could muster, she called for her husband, "Scott!"

Of course she knew he could not hear her.

She yelled in a labored voice, "I need help! I can't get it fixed! God, please let him somehow know I need him!"

Darnisha's constant kicking to stay afloat was depleting her strength. Israfel shouted passed the confusion in her mind, "Manually fill your vest!"

The thought from Israfel finally reached her, "Fill the vest manually so that you can float."

"But, I don't know if I can. I'm too tired," She said aloud to herself.

By this time, her strength was so depleted and she was breathing hard. She pressed the very stiff manual inflate button and blew with all her might. She couldn't get any air into the BC. "Oh, no!" With rations of her last energy, she kicked up out of the water, just like she was trained, depressed the button, and with one more attempt, blew as hard as she could but with no avail. Dezro was there cheering her failed attempt.

Anxiety and a horrifying sense of being totally alone settled into her heart and mind.

"Scott!" she screamed.

"He can't hear me!" She said franticly.

She grabbed her knife and tapped her tank in hopes that he could hear the ping underwater.

No luck.

"What am I going to do? Jesus, help me think."

"I have to relax and swim to the ledge," she reasoned. "Where is the truck?"

She strained to scan the distant shore. As she squinted, she could see a white shape in the distance. It was the truck.

"If I can find the ledge, I can stand up. Just swim. Relax and swim."

She was more fearful now as she started to swim. She coached herself for the journey. "You have plenty of air, Darnisha. Just swim to the ledge."

Realizing that navigation had somehow been overtly difficult today, she reminded herself, "Swim straight, don't swim out deeper. Jesus, please help me not to go the wrong direction!"

She put her face into the water and kicked. She couldn't see the bottom of the lake.

It was so cloudy.

The feeling of being lost and alone flooded in.

"Scott, where are you? I need you. Please come up. God, please tell him to come up. I need help."

She noticed that for some reason, she kept drifting on an angle away from the shore.

Darnisha thought that the currents must have changed. In fact, it was the work of several demons as they playfully pushed her off course. Nonetheless, she put her head down and continued to try and swim.

"Lord, please let me swim straight! PLEASE!"

Panic had already taken hold of her and the ability to think rationally was gone. Darnisha did her best to swim as she struggled to get air but swallowed gulps of water instead. Somehow, she barely noticed.

After several minutes of kicking, she lifted her head again to be sure that she was still on course.

"OH, NO, I'm swimming toward the middle of the lake. OH, MY GOD!," she cried.

The thought hit her, "I can't believe that I'm going to die like this."

Drowning had always been Darnisha's most feared way of dying.

"JESUS!! JESUS!!! JESUS!!!! If you don't help me, I'm not going to make it!" she screamed.

"Scott won't be able to find me in this water. Oh, God, help my husband. He'll have to tell my family. He'll have to tell everyone."

She struggled to turn over and swim on her back. "Maybe I'll relax this way."

As she rolled over and looked into the sky for what she thought would be the last time, all she felt so alone.

She thought, "There's no one, no life out here. No one can hear me." There was an unnatural quiet and desolation across the lake.

In these quiet final moments, instead of seeing her past life flash before her eyes, she flashed forward and could see the future. She saw her husband in tears. She saw her pink casket and memorial service. Then the sobering thought hit her, "I will never lead worship again."

As Darnisha cried out to her Savior in fear, Israfel watched in tears as she continued to fight off the provoking demons. Israfel ached for her as she watched Darnisha struggle to hold onto her life...her Darnisha. Israfel could barely keep herself from grabbing her and taking her from this place; she wanted so badly to let her know it was going to be all right. But Israfel had instructions, "Allow this to happen."

Darnisha, too tired to fight much longer, talked to God saying, "Lord, let me see a bird; there is no living thing here. Please let me see something alive once more."

Immediately, the Escorter of prayers shot to the throne of God and within seconds of man's time the keepers of the wind alerted a sparrow flying over the lake. It crossed right over Darnisha.

The guardian looked up and said, "What love Almighty God has for his children." She smiled and looked back down at Darnisha and said, "Yes, Child, He knows where His sparrows are and He is certainly watching you, my love…it is time to leave this world, for now."

Dezro regained his wits, realized the job was not done. He turned his attention to Scott. "Come on, let's go for both of them," he shouted! With another cry of victory, Dezro darted towards Scott.

Scott started towards the surface.

He found it difficult to maintain his slow ascent rate. Everything was murky.

By now, he just wanted to get away from the eerie shadows and to find Darnisha.

Feeling terribly concerned, Scott opted to skip his safety stop. He knew that he should take one but it had been too long since Darnisha's ascent.

He broke the surface of the water.

"Where is she?" Darnisha was nowhere to be found.

Scott spun completely around in the water, "Darnisha!" he shouted.

"Where did she go?"

"She must have started back down as I was coming up. The water was so murky that we could have passed each other and not known."

Scott scanned the surface for air bubbles. In the cloudy water it would be almost impossible to find her without a reference.

"No air bubbles."

Just then, he noticed off in the distance something very small break the surface of the water. "What is that?" He couldn't tell what it was. As he looked more intently, he realized that the object was metal. It was the top of Darnisha's air tank.

"Oh my goodness, it's Darnisha!"

Dezro placed selfish thoughts into Scott's mind to throw him off.

"Now why would she just abandon me, on the bottom of the lake?"

"Why would she just swim off and leave me here? Thanks a lot."

Scott felt betrayed and hurt.

"She just took off swimming for the shore and left me waiting for her on the bottom of the lake." Scott shouted to her, "Darnisha! Darnisha what are you doing?!"

She did not respond.

Dezro continued his mind games with Scott, turning hurt to anger.

As Scott started swimming towards her, he angrily yelled out to her,

"Darnisha! Hey, what the heck are you doing?!"

Just then, Scott could see she wasn't swimming; she was fighting to stay on the surface.

Israfel watched Darnisha gasp for breath. She became perplexed at what she observed next. Darnisha was surrendering her life. Israfel was astonished. This physical being was able to see beyond her physical pain and the incredible drive for life and had surrendered her body to the Lord. A new prayer entered into the spirit realm.

Still conscious, suddenly Darnisha became calm. Her erratic movement stopped. She stopped crying out. She rolled over to put her face back into the water and prayed her final prayer,

"Father, Thy will be done. If this is what you have for me, I trust you. I trust you to take care of my dear husband and my family. Forgive me of all my sin. Just help me to swim straight." She rested her face into the water and drifted away peacefully.

"She's drowning!" Scott thought.

"Darnisha, I'm coming!", was no sooner out of his mouth than Scott could see only the top of her hands above the water, then nothing.

"Oh No, Oh God, Darnisha I'm coming!!" Scott screamed.

Immediately, he took a bearing from where he had last seen her, dropped below the surface, and started swimming as hard as he could.

Israfel put Darnisha's mind to sleep as her body took its last breath.

A shout was heard as Dezro and his fellow tormentors began to celebrate their victory. "She's dead! We did it!!" Dezro shouted in excitement and disbelief. "I can't believe it! We did it!" Great excitement grew deep in his black heart.

"I will be celebrated. This will be the beginning of the conquests of Dezro!"

Dezro's head swelled with pride.

Israfel carefully cradled Darnisha's soul, carrying her to the crossing place of the spirit realm. As an heir, Darnisha would be given an opportunity to choose to stay in the life she was living on earth or to walk through the transition place into eternity. Israfel knew she would have to keep Darnisha distracted from that decision. She had her assignment to keep Darnisha from deciding to transition from the physical life to eternal life.

She's Gone

"What happened? How did she get so far away?"

He just couldn't believe this was happening. It was like living a nightmare.

Scott swam as hard as he could but it didn't feel like he was moving at all. It was like those terrible dreams where everything is in slow motion.

Enoch fought hard to keep Dezro and his demons away from Scott.

As Dezro fed thoughts into Scott's mind, the others did all they could to alter his course towards his wife. As the demons continued to cause Scott to stray off course, they mocked Enoch's efforts.

With this, Enoch pulled out his flaming sword and wielded it effortlessly yet with precision. In a fraction of a mortal's heartbeat both demons were vaporized and faded into nothingness.

Dezro, losing his blockers, screamed out for more help as he continued to hurl confusion into Scott's mind.

"Oh please, God, let her be all right," Scott prayed over and over again.

"Where is she?!" He was starting to hyperventilate by now.

His body was nearing exhaustion from swimming so hard against the current and cold. He felt light-headed.

The water was looking black in his peripheral vision.

He realized he was reaching his physical limits.

With one more guiding assist, Enoch directed Scott to his bride's body still a good distance away. Scott pressed forward. At the moment he thought he couldn't go any longer, he saw a dark shadow outlined in the water ahead of him and slowly drifting downward.

"Thank God, I found her!" he thought.

As he got closer to the shadow, he could see Darnisha's back was towards him.

He then saw what brought chills to his spine... it was the dark shadowy outline of her regulator floating alongside her.

His body tingled as if all his blood was drained from him.

He quickly grabbed his secondary regulator and held it in front of him as he swam toward her. He reached out with his right hand to grab her and swing her around to face him. He started to put the regulator into her mouth.

Terror went through his soul. "Oh, God. I'm too late."

Her eyes were wide open and rolled back into her head.

Her mouth was open and full of water.

She was gone.

In a complete panic, he grabbed her and pulled her lifeless body to the surface. He ripped the regulator out of his mouth and started shouting her name.

"DARNISHA!! DARNISHA!! Please, Baby, come on! Talk to me! Come on, Honey!" He started shaking her, shouting her name.

"Come on, Darnisha! Come back to me! Come on!"

Desperately, he pulled her mask off her face. As Scott tread the water, he struggled to keep her on the surface. She was dead weight.

He was still too far out to stand up but he had to do something.

He wrapped one arm around her waist to hold her and with his free arm he tried to take her gear off.

She folded in half, bending backward with her face back into the water.

Her eyes still open and mouth filling again with water. He stopped and pulled her up.

Still treading water, he tried to inflate her BC manually. Again she bent backward and her head fell below the water's surface.

"DARNISHA! Please, Baby, come back!"

Dezro smiled, chuckled, and then folded into hysterical laughter.

"You are too late, guardian!" She's gone. Now I am going to destroy your boy!

Into Eternity

The small Chinese woman, still in her homemade red pantsuit, opened her eyes.

She found herself kneeling in a place more peaceful, restful than any place she had ever been.

She noticed immediately that tranquility permeated all of her senses.

She was even aware of senses she had never known before.

Complete joy flowed through her body.

As she stood to her feet, she noticed that she felt light. Like she had been carrying an unseen weight all her life that was now lifted.

It was wonderful!

As her eyes focused to the brightness, she could see all kinds of people walking in intersecting lines.

She tried to take in all that was happening but her eyes were drawn to a radiant light to her right.

As she looked more intently, she realized that it was a magnificent winged being standing just behind a specific woman who was kneeling.

The small Chinese woman turned to check but she did not have an escort.

"I wonder who that woman is? She must be someone important. She doesn't look like the rest of us. Our time has clearly come," she thought to herself.

Israfel, standing behind Darnisha, touched her gently on her shoulder awaking her.

Darnisha opened her eyes and found herself kneeling in a place she had never been before. But somehow, it felt like she was home.

She was in the crossing.

The crossing is the transition place for souls newly departed from their physical body.

It is wide-open space with wall-less boundaries of brilliant expanse, clean and bright.

Darnisha felt as if she were taking her very first breath of life giving air.

The guardian began to give her instruction.

"Now that you're here…"

Darnisha was too taken in by her new surroundings. She only heard that someone was talking to her, but not a word they were saying. She was fascinated with the countless people filing into inter crossing lines in front of her. It was so complex, yet it made perfect sense.

"Where am I?" she thought.

The guardian allowed Darnisha to be sidetracked.

She was trying to take in all the aspects of this foreign place. She was clearly captivated by the endless amount of souls on their way to their eternal destination.

Everybody was dressed as they would have been if you had seen them on the street.

They each looked purposeful and content about their direction.

Even though the lines were going several directions, they all seemed to flow in harmony.

"I must be in a place where souls in the balance," Darnisha reasoned.

She could see that for some souls it was not their time to cross and they would return to their physical bodies. The many lines went through one massive glimmering opening then funneled into two distinct lines.

As they continued on, the two lines drifted further apart.

The people who moved along in the line to the left seemed to become more and more weighed down. They began to slouch and their countenance saddened with each step.

One by one, the weight overwhelming each person bringing them to tears.

Still, in all this activity, Darnisha had never felt so peaceful, so rested.

As she realized that instructions were still being given to her, she tried to focus. She heard.

"If you choose to enter the line, you cannot return."

"I have a choice?" she asked.

"What should I do? I like it here. I want to see what's beyond the line. But should I?" she questioned within herself.

Just then, the Chinese woman stood up from her kneeling place and began walking forward. The prompting toward her purposed line was so great that every earthly memory became dim.

Darnisha noticed her beautiful outfit and jet black hair as soon as she stood.

However, just before the Chinese woman took her place in line and onto her eternal destiny, she felt an overwhelming urge to speak to the woman with the guardian.

As she crossed in front of Darnisha still on her knees, the Chinese woman stood in front of her.

She stopped, looked down, and smiled.

She said, "My sister, you don't belong here now. It is not your time. You must go back."

With those words she bowed, turned, and merged effortlessly into her line. With her final assignment complete, she moved forward feeling more joy and tranquility with each step. She could see something in the distance, a brilliantly bright light. She had a hard time containing her soul's excitement.

HELP US!

As Scott continued to struggle with his wife's lifeless body, he realized that with all the classes and training he had taken in scuba, he had never taken a CPR class.

"What am I going to do!!?

I don't know what to do," he cried out in despair.

"JESUS!!! PLEASE HELP ME!!!"

Enoch gave Scott's prayer to a messenger angel.

The messenger rocketed to the throne room of God. Running towards the throne, he was met by the concerned Son of God.

Immediately the messenger dropped to his knees.

"Jesus! Your child is crying out for assistance!"

Just then God the Father turned his face toward the messenger and His Son.

"Darnisha is at the crossing, Almighty God," the messenger said.

The God of creation turned his glance past the messenger.

Looking off into time itself, He was silent for a moment before responding, "Do nothing."

"Tell them to do nothing, my Lord?", the messenger asked with great confusion.

"No. Do not respond."

Jesus turned to look at the throne and the radiant presence of God the Father.

"Nothing, Father?

Can we minister to his spirit and give him confidence that you are at work?"

"We shall not give any answer or any confidence that we have even heard his prayer or are working on his behalf."

Jesus' head bent downward as he turned back to the messenger.

"Thus sayeth the Lord,"

Jesus proclaimed with great concern and anguish.

"What do I do, Lord?" the messenger asked puzzled.

"Go back to him but don't allow your presence to be felt. Don't intervene for him. Just watch over him and carry this memory reminder to him."

Jesus handed the messenger what appeared to be a small sphere of radiant light.

The messenger took it and placed it into his satchel.

"Tell Enoch to keep watch and keep the enemy at bay until it is completed."

"Praise Your Name," the messenger said as he stood, bowed before Jesus and The Almighty God.

He then turned and walked out of the throne room and speedily made his way back to Scott in the physical realm.

"I have to get her to breathe," Scott said, nearly out of breath himself.

Just then the tormenting demons hurled more negative thoughts and lies at him.

They screamed,

"She's gone! There's nothing you can do about it. It's your entire fault. You killed her!"

Over and over again, the demons shouted into Scott's thoughts.

"NO! NO! DARNISHA!! Baby, please come back!"

Just then, the messenger arrived back from the throne room of God.

Enoch looked at him with anxious anticipation, waiting for a word to relay to Scott's soul.

"Our Lord said to do nothing"

Enoch's heart sank. As his mind raced to figure out what to do, the messenger reached into his satchel and pulled out a glittering memory reminder and handed it to Enoch.

Enoch held it up to his face. The memory jumped into his mind. As Enoch saw the memory, he smiled and whispered, "Thank you, Jesus." Then placed it into Scott's mind.

A flash of light captured Scott's mind muting the demonic insults.

It was an image from a movie he loved. A scene from the movie "The Abyss." His mind's eye could see how the main characters, husband and wife, were trapped in a mini-sub that was floating just 50 yards from their underwater base. In the movie, they didn't have enough air supply for both of them to get to safety. So, the wife decided to allow herself to drown so that her husband could revive her once he reached the base with her body in tow. Her husband pulled her lifeless body to the base and quickly started CPR.

Scott couldn't think rationally about much, but somehow he could see this scene clearly in his mind. He started imitating what he saw.

He couldn't hold Darnisha's nose because one arm was already wrapped around her waist to keep her on the surface.

He grabbed her head and pulled her close.

He put his lips on hers and blew. When the air come out, he did it again.

This time when the air came out it was accompanied by a spine-tingling gurgle, lungs full of water.

"Oh, God. No," he thought.

He had heard of this before but until now had never experienced it.

It was horrible and defeating. His confidence in any likelihood of success was quickly diminishing.

Dezro's voice broke into Scott's mind again and relentlessly ripped apart his hope.

"You killed her with your stupid sport. You had three good weeks with her, but she is gone now."

"NO! Baby, please breathe!" Scott punched her chest with all his might to try to pump her heart.

He looked up towards shore and thought, "I need to get to shore." As he continued CPR, he attempted to swim towards the truck, still a good 600 yards away.

He blew in her mouth again and let the air come back out. Still there was no response.

"She is gone; just let her go. Everyone is going to blame you and hate you for getting her into this stupid sport. You killed her and her parents will try to prosecute you for killing her."

"NO! NO! She cannot be gone."

Scott was in turmoil as he thought, "Is this true, is this what God has planned for us?"

Enoch immediately answered his question by flooding his mind with more memories and prophecies of the couple's life together.

In this moment of chaos, Scott scanned over the memories of his relationship with his new wife. Enoch highlighted one in particular. The calling that the couple felt together from God to go to a place on faith they did not know, a place where he would use them in ministry.

"This is not the end. God has promised too many things to us, our life together. We're going to move to California and work together.

We cannot be finished!

NO, I WILL NOT GIVE UP!!!" Scott found new determination. He continued breathing for Darnisha and punching her chest.

"Please someone, HELP! HELP!"

As he shouted, he glanced around the lake. There was not a soul in sight anywhere on the lake or even on the shore. He felt utterly alone and exhausted.

His strength was almost depleted

By this time, Scott was struggling to keep himself on the surface as well.

"It's taking too long," Enoch worriedly spoke aloud.

"Messenger, tell Jesus they are not here yet. It is taking too long. Tell him the Carmichaels are not here yet. Ask what do I do."

"Yes Enoch, be strong,"

The messenger responded as he shot back to the omnipotent God's throne room.

One Coming Back, One Staying

The messenger, now back in the throne room frantically called on the name of Jesus.

"Savior of man, it is taking too long. Her body will be damaged. Her mind. Lord, her lungs, her voice, her instrument of praise will be damaged."

The Lord Jesus, Son of the living God, grabbed his chest, his eyes filled with unbearable pain.

"Oh my dear darling child," came out of his mouth in a whisper of agony as if the ordeal were happening to him.

Jesus had always loved watching His Father enjoy the praises that flowed from the heart of His daughter, Darnisha.

Jesus turned to His father seated on his throne.

"Father, will this be allowed to happen?"

Before the question was finished being asked, a determined response left the mouth of God.

"No, she will not experience damage to her body.

She will make it through this deathgate.

Then, my son, you can send healing through your spirit.

There will not be a trace of this incident anywhere in her body."

The small Chinese woman could see that her line was headed between two magnificent white pearl columns. There was nothing beyond the columns but radiant light.

So bright was the light that she could not see the line of people who had passed beyond the columns. They simply disappeared.

The line was moving faster now. She noticed that her momentum was not coming from her feet.

Two enormous angelic beings with flaming swords stood in front of each column.

The next thing she knew, she was at the front of the line only steps away from passing through to the other side of the columns.

To her right, just this side of the columns, was another angelic being. Not as large as the others, but still much larger than she. He stood in front of a crystal podium with a large ancient book on it.

He looked at her closely then turned to the book. Filing through several pages, he scrolled down one side of a page. She could see his eyes stop and fix on what he was looking for. A smile came to his face. He looked straight into her eyes and spoke her name and said,

"Welcome home. The Savior has been waiting for you." With that, he gestured to her that it was all right to walk beyond the columns. She smiled back and with great excitement stepped through.

Faster than a blink and with the sound of a rushing wind, she was transported through the amazing light.

She closed her eye for the brightness, and suddenly it was quiet again. The light was not overwhelming anymore, but now she could feel warmth on her face.

Opening her eyes, she found herself standing in the gardens of paradise. It was beyond what she could have ever possibly imagined. She took a deep breath as if it were her first. As she inhaled, she could feel this new air dance throughout her body and regenerate her very soul.

As she attempted to take in the breathtakingly beautiful landscape that surrounded her, she saw a tall man walking towards her.

She had never seen Him before but somehow even at a distance, she knew Him intimately.

As He came closer she could see an amazing smile across His radiant face.

She began to tremble.

She bowed her head in reverence.

As He came closer, she could feel His presence. She felt a gentle touch on her chin, lifting her face.

She looked up directly into the kindest, most compassionate, and deeply loving eyes she had ever seen. She began to cry. "My Jesus," she spoke in a whisper.

He smiled and said, "Yes, NuWang. I have been waiting for you. Your life has pleased me greatly. Well done, my daughter."

NuWang began to weep with joy as the Savior of the world, the Son of the Almighty God, put his arms around her and wept with her.

"I Have to Go Back!"

"Oh, I need to pay attention to what this person is saying to me," Darnisha thought.

"I'm sorry, I wasn't really listening.

Now, what am I supposed to be doing again?"

Israfel, Darnisha's guardian, began the entire speech again for her.

"Now that you're here, you need to…" At that moment Darnisha felt a sharp pain go through her body.

"Ouch. What is that?

Stop it! Leave me alone!

Ouch! Stop it! Stop it. It hurts."

She yelled with all her might. She screamed at the top of her lungs, because the pain was intense.

"Why is someone messing with me? Stop it! What's happening?"

The pain completely weakened her spirit. Just then, everything went black and Darnisha remembered what was happening before she entered her peaceful place.

She realized what had happened in the lake. Still floating in the quietness of her mind she said to herself, "Darnisha, stop fighting him.

You have to go back. Relax and let him bring you back." She could hear her own voice echo across the realms beyond the physical world.

In the cold murky water of Crystal Lake, Scott blew another breath into his wife. As the air left her body, there was a low groan. He couldn't tell if it was her making the sound or if it was just air passing over her vocal chords. Now ten minutes into kicking as hard as he could to keep them afloat, he blew again and waited for the air to come back out.

"Baby, is that you?" he asked with cautious hope.

This time there was another groan but more prolonged and long after the air had exited her lungs.

"It *is* you!"

By now, the adrenalin surging through Scott's body was used up. He was starting to sink. His strength was gone and he was still nowhere near where he could stand up and support both of them.

Hope Appears

Armed with new reinforcements for the battle, Dezro continued to work hard on Scott's thoughts affecting his emotions. He pulled out a cloak of isolation and wrapped Scott in it.

Scott felt an utter sense of abandonment. Not just physically alone, but he felt spiritually abandoned.

"Where are you, God?"

"Jesus! Jesus! Jesus!"

Scott had the dreadful realization that they were alone on the lake.

There was no one to see or hear his frantic screams.

Scott cried out louder, "Jesus! Jesus! Help me!! Please!" he pleaded.

He was physically exhausted.

He began to fear that his own ability to continue was fading. His strength was utterly depleted.

Scott thought that his relationship with God, his growing ability to hear his voice and sense His promptings, would cause him to feel some sort of supernatural presence, superhuman strength.

Some sign from God to help him through this living nightmare.

But there was nothing…at least nothing that could be felt or seen by a physical being.

In fact, God was at work.

Scott was completely unaware of the monumental battle that was being fought on his behalf in the spirit realm.

The voice of the Father spoke through the fabric of creation,

"Open his eyes, Enoch, let him see."

Enoch cleared Scott's vision.

In that moment, Scott looked up to the east and saw a small white boat coming towards him.

He frantically waved his free arm to get attention.

The boat was almost to the first dive flag that Scott had placed at the couple's entry point.

"Watch out, Patrick. There must be divers in the water," Peggy shouted from the back of the small white boat as she spotted the dive flag ahead of them in the water.

"I see it," Patrick replied.

As he was piloting the boat along in the now much calmer waters he noticed another spot of red. Standing up and squinting, he could make out a second dive flag straight ahead of them.

He jerked the steering wheel to the right and the boat made an abrupt turn south.

"Wow, another one. Girls, help me keep an eye out for this group. There must be more than one of them out here."

"Ok," the ladies chimed.

Just a few hundred yards from the boat, Scott waved frantically at them.

The boat was nearly parallel with the couple now.

Patrick announced, "Hey, check out the divers to the left." Jacqueline and Peggy stopped their conversation and turned towards the shore. After a moment of scanning the water surface, they too caught a glimpse of the black figure waving.

"There he is!", announced Patrick as they all waved back. "Hi!!!!"

"They waved to me! Oh No, they think I am just waving to them!" Scott began to panic.

"I have to do something else to get them to come over to us." So he curled his arm and brought it to the top of his head. He did this very quickly and repeatedly hoping they could see he needed attention.

Scott knew if he didn't get them to see that they needed help, their chances for survival would disappear.

Just then Scott heard the roar of the engine get quiet.

The boat abruptly turned toward him and the body of his bride.

"Thank God!! They are coming," he desperately reassured himself.

Darnisha, though, was still not responding. He had no idea what had happened and why she had aborted the dive.

Scott didn't know if she had an air embolism, a problem surfacing, or if the equipment failed.

All of these unanswered questions were bombarding his mind. But he couldn't think of that right now. He held Darnisha and continued to struggle keeping them both afloat until their rescuers came.

As the boat drew closer, Scott began to make out three people. He could see the concern on all their faces.

As the trio carefully eased their way toward the couple, they saw a worried man holding in his arms a motionless woman.

Jacqueline gasped and whispered, "Oh, my God," and immediately started to pray.

The words of that prayer were carried on the wind by Jacqueline's guardian and whisked past Scott's ears before launching to the throne room of Almighty God.

When Scott heard it, hope sparked deep within his now frantic heart.

Dezro felt his grip loosen as power from the Spirit jolted through Scott's body and mind.

Scott shouted out,

"We had a diving accident. When I found her she wasn't breathing. She still isn't responding to me."

Immediately, Patrick swung the boat around so that he could access the divers and quickly shut the engine off.

"Are you OK? Don't worry, we'll get you out of here," Jacqueline consoled.

As Peggy and Jacqueline reassured Scott that everything would be all right now, Patrick reached down and grabbed Darnisha by the arms. Her body responded like a wet noodle and he couldn't lift up the dead weight.

"Let's get her equipment off so I can lift her in. OK?" Patrick said to Scott.

So, Patrick held her against the boat as Scott remained in the water and began to take off her dive gear.

Scott peeled off her BC and air tank and tried to hand it to the ladies on the boat.

He was so tired that the gear kept pulling him under.

His arms were so weak by now he couldn't lift the equipment.

Tired of fighting with it, he decided to let it go and drop it.

The equipment quickly sank out of sight as it headed to the murky bottom of the lake.

Patrick quickly found a rope and ran it under both of Darnisha's arms. He and Jacqueline, using the rope as a pulley, attempted to hoist her out of the water.

They were able to keep her on the surface but still couldn't get her into the boat.

Frustrated, Patrick said, "Let's get her to the back of the boat on the swim platform."

The group guided Darnisha's body to the back of the boat with the ropes from the boat and Scott still holding her in the water.

With his final bit of strength, and all the help of their rescuers, Scott lifted Darnisha onto the swim platform.

Just as her torso cleared the water, she began coughing up water that had filled her lungs, the immediately, the content of her stomach. Scott, now just below her in the water, was the target for the upheaval.

Just then, Darnisha woke from the shadows of her grave. She slowly began to make out the white boat she was now on and three blurry strangers frantically attempting to get her into the boat

She saw her husband panting and talking to one of the new strangers about getting her out of the water.

She thought to herself that she should try to help them, but she couldn't make her body move.

With the little strength she had, she slowly turned her head towards her husband's ear and whispered, "Sorry."

The whisper startled and relieved Scott. It was the first he had heard Darnisha speak since the dive began nearly an hour ago.

"It's OK, Baby," he comforted her.

The dark-haired Jacqueline saw that Scott was visibly shaken and in shock, "Are you doing, OK, Hon?"

Scott returned a shaky, "I'm Okay."

I'm just glad she's finally breathing. I'm not sure if she can move."

He was still in the water holding onto the swim ladder.

Jacqueline, Patrick, and Peggy got Darnisha the rest of the way onto the boat and lying on the rear bench seat.

Jacqueline turning her attention to Scott, said, "Come on, you'd better get that gear off and get in the boat, too."

He took his gear off and handed it up to Jacqueline.

She could barely lift it.

"How in the world could you stay afloat with all this weight on?" she asked.

"I don't know. I almost didn't. If you all hadn't come when you did, we both would have died today," Scott said with a sobering calm.

With great effort, Jacqueline pulled his equipment into the boat. Then she stretched out a hand to help Scott into the boat.

With shaky arms, he hoisted himself on to the swim platform. Still shaken, he knelt there for a moment, resting all his weight on the rear seat.

"You must be exhausted! How long were you struggling?" Jacqueline asked him.

"I don't really know," Scott responded in a daze.

"Let me get you a drink." Peggy said.

She pulled out a two liter orange pop and poured some into a plastic cup.

Handing it to Scott, he drank it all in one gulp.

Peggy looked down at his hands and noticed that he was shaking like a leaf.

"We've got to get you two to the hospital," she said with great concern.

"I'm all right." Scott replied, "If you could just get us to my truck I can drive her to the hospital."

They all agreed as Scott pointed towards his truck on the shore.

Patrick turned the engine back on and they headed in.

The ladies were still trying to get Darnisha to talk to them. They kept asking, "What is your name?"

Darnisha's mind was fuzzy and still was unable to process information or control her body yet.

She tried to talk, but could not get her thoughts and words to work together. She just lay still with her mind a blur looking at her husband who looked like he had just been through a battle.

Scott was still worried.

He didn't know if she had brain damage or was she paralyzed.

"She's still not moving," Scott said.

"Can you move, Babe?" he kept asking Darnisha.

As hard as she tried, Darnisha could not respond, except with infrequent and faint whispers.

"Let's get that wet suite off and get her dry," Jacqueline said.

She and Peggy struggled to take the skin-tight wetsuit off Darnisha's still limp body. As soon as they loosened the zipper, blood began flowing through Darnisha's body.

She could feel her limbs again and moved her legs. "Oh, she moved! Good girl!" Peggy said with joy.

"Thank God!" Scott said, feeling somewhat consoled.

That was one huge concern Scott had that was now gone.

As they got her wet suite off and wrapped her in a towel, Scott cradled Darnisha. She whispered,

"I want to go home."

"OK, Baby. I'll take you home.

Don't worry. You're all right now."

His heart felt like it started to beat again.

The dark-haired woman said to Scott, "By the way, my name is Jacqueline. This is my husband, Patrick, and our friend, Peggy."

Scott introduced himself and Darnisha. "We've just been married three weeks now," he said.

"This wasn't your honeymoon was it?" Patrick asked.

"No. This was supposed to be a romantic weekend.

So much for that," Scott dryly stated.

"Well, God was sure looking out for you today!" Jacqueline declared.

"Yes," Scott replied, "You are our angels; that's for sure."

Patrick pulled back on the throttle. As they approached the shore, the water started to get very shallow. He shut the engine off as Scott jumped out of the boat and ran to shore to get the truck.

Scott grabbed the keys out of their hiding place in the Reese hitch, hit the door lock button on the remote, and jumped into the truck.

He quickly started the Yukon and reached down and pulled a leaver that engaged the four-wheel drive, then shifted the truck into drive. Scott turned the truck around and aimed it towards the waiting boat just off shore and hit the gas.

The truck leaped forward with all four tires digging into the loose gravel parking lot. The truck launched down the short but steep decent into the lake. The Yukon did not lose momentum as it splashed into the lake and gripped into the lake bed, still on course for the waiting boat now just a dozen yards away.

Fortunately, the lake had very shallow beaches and by the time Scott had reached the boat, the water was only touching the bottom of the truck's door frames.

He pulled parallel to the boat; close enough for them to carry Darnisha from the boat directly to the back seat of the SUV.

Scott, Patrick, and Peggy hoisted Darnisha into the back of the truck, while Jacqueline steadied the boat. Once Darnisha was situated in the back seat, Peggy announced, "I will ride with them back to the dock so we can give them the map from my car." She jumped into the front passenger seat.

Scott waded into the water once again to push the boat containing Patrick and Jacqueline out into deeper water. Patrick started the engine and quickly headed back to their dock. Scott joined Peggy and Darnisha in the truck and drove it out of the lake. Soon the truck was crawling up the steep embankment, and across the gravel parking lot.

Following Peggy's directions, he turned right onto the main road and headed back towards the village where Patrick and Jacqueline docked their boat.

Peggy kept talking to Darnisha to make sure she was still responsive.

"She's doing just fine," she reassured Scott who was still shaken.

"And you are in full protection mode, aren't you?" she asked and tried gently get Scott to realize.

"I'm sure. I've just got to get her to the doctor to make sure she's OK. I'll feel better then."

Several minutes passed before they pulled into downtown Beulah and found Patrick and Jacqueline walking towards their car.

Scott pulled up next to their car and rolled down his window. Jacqueline walked over and said, "We have decided we are going to take you to the hospital."

"No, I'm fine; I can make it, no problem," Scott nervously responded. He didn't realize what he was declining at the time.

Peggy jumped out of the truck and ran over to her parked car. She grabbed the map out of her glove box and brought it to Scott.

She pulled out a pen and highlighted the best way to the hospital. "Now, here is where you're headed. And this is the fastest route." Are you sure you're OK to do this on your own?" The route was full of twists and turns. Too complicated for anyone in the wrong state of mind.

"Yeah, this is about a 45 minute drive. We're more than happy to take you," Jacqueline insisted.

"Really, I think I'll be all right. You all have done so much already," Scott replied with adrenaline-filled confidence. He was anxious to get his bride to the doctor and did not want to waste any time making travel arrangements.

He gave them each a hug and promised he would call to let them know how everything turned out.

He swiftly drove through the small village and turned north onto the main road to find the Traverse City Hospital.

"She's back and they have made it through the deathgate," one of the demons sorrowfully proclaimed.

Dezro screamed in agony, "No, no, no!" In an uncontrollable rage, he gritted his fangs and raised his clenched fists. He shouted to the legion of demons clinging to the now-completed gateway, "No! It is not over; follow me!"

With heads hung low, the defeated legion of demons could not look at the irate Dezro, nor had any hope or will to continue the fight.

Dezro shouted again, "Come on, there is still a chance! We can get them!"

There was no response from Dezro's colleagues other than turning away from his glare. His hope for revenge began to fade.

Just then, a battle screech of two vile demons could be heard from the top of the now-powerless deathgate.

Dezro smirked as he took flight with his two recruits.

"We are not defeated yet!" Dezro screamed as the evil trio flew toward the Taylor's truck.

The Battle to the Hospital

Sitting silently behind the wheel of his SUV, Scott's adrenaline slowly diminished. His mind began to clear and process what had just happened.

"I should have let them drive us to the hospital," he repeated over again to himself. The complexity of the trip to the nearest hospital began to create a new anxiety as he drove through the twists and turns of the back-country roads.

Every minute he would glance back and check Darnisha, still lying across the back seat.

"Are you still with me, Babe?"

He continually reached back and would give her a little shake.

"Darnisha? Babe?" he repeated to get her to respond.

Darnisha still felt very weak and foggy as she lay still

"Huh?"

"Uh, ha," was all she could muster.

Scott angled his rearview mirror down so he could watch her and make sure she was breathing.

Her grunting responses were all he needed for now.

He wouldn't feel completely at ease until he heard the doctor's prognosis. She was alive, yes, but had he gotten to her in time?

"Oh, God. Please let her be all right."

He still didn't know what caused the accident.

He was terrified that she had a lung injury or worse, brain damage.

She was out so long. This new fear haunted his thoughts as he frantically sped along the now-dark winding roads.

Enoch was busy directing Scott's attention back to the road. Scott was so distracted with his new bride that he kept veering and swerving over the center yellow line and off the shoulder.

Israfel watched over Darnisha, speaking peace into her raw spirit freshly back in her body.

Nothing was real yet for her. She felt she was still hovering somewhere between the physical and spiritual.

As Israfel softly sang to Darnisha, black-cloaked streaks heading toward the truck caught her attention.

"Enoch, they're coming!" Israfel shouted as Dezro and his companions landed on the roof of the SUV and began crawling into the cabin.

Israfel drew her flaming sword and began to fight off the evil warriors.

Dezro slithered passed Israfel, who had her hands full with his demon recruits. He quickly maneuvered past Enoch who had his hands full keeping Scott focused on the road. Dezro took his place into Scott's fragile mind hurling accusations and confusion.

"She's going to be damaged for life and it's all your fault. Why did you let her do this? You did everything wrong, you know that! You always do everything WRONG!"

Like a jellyfish's long tentacles, Dezro reached into Scott's mind engulfing it as he began to poison his soul. Too quick for Enoch to grab, Dezro slithered down Scott's spinal cord and attached himself to his nervous system. Here Dezro unleashed a flood of disturbing images.

Under normal circumstances, it would have been a beautiful drive to Traverse City. The sun was getting low in the west. Nature was peaceful… in the physical realm, but in the spirit realm, the battle continued.

Scott gripped the steering wheel tight with his right hand, the map in his left.

He kept checking and watching for street names in the complex route to the hospital.

He battled against the confusion and disturbing thoughts as Dezro continued bombarding his mind.

Scott was driving much too fast for the type of roads they were traveling.

"Where is a cop when you really want one?!" he thought.

"I should have let them drive us…or should I have called the ambulance?…or at least the police! How stupid."

Dezro, now nestled into a weak spot, continued to hurl evil saturated fistfuls of doubt and turmoil as Enoch attempted to deflect them away.

Scott was second-guessing everything now.

"Oh, I just missed my next turn!" as Scott blazed by the road.

He hit the brakes hard and turned into a nearby drive.

Israfel continued her attack on the demons wielding her flaming sword as the battle continued back to the truck's roof.

One of the demons launched himself towards her screaming blasphemies as he swung his blackened battle-axe overhead.

With the speed of lightning, the guardian swung her sword at the air-born demon and severed his putrid body in two.

The charred pieces fell, sizzling from the cauterizing heat, then became ash and blew away with the wind.

The other demon screamed as he tackled Israfel, pinning her to the truck's roof.

It laughed and with a sickening groan leaned his rotting face towards her beautiful one.

With all of hell's perversion, he stuck his tongue out to lick her angelic face.

Just before his decaying puss-covered tongue reached her face, he froze as if he had been turned into stone.

His beady black eyes opened wide as he stared into the now fiery eyes of Israfel.

His lustful groan quickly turned to one of agony as Israfel pulled the small dagger out of the chest of the demon and returned it to her belt. With one fluid move, Israfel launched the stunned demon into the air with her legs. As the demon's body crashed to the road behind the speeding truck, the withered carcass like his predecessor exploded into ash.

"How could you have let her go to the surface alone?" Dezro continued to jeer, "You and your stupid hobby! Why wasn't it you? You're the one who takes all the risks!"

Scott was losing control.

Enoch, full of holy rage, grabbed Dezro with one hand around his bony twisted neck and pulled him and his buried tentacles out of Scott and away from the driver's seat.

He lifted him high above his head and raised his angelic sword. Dezro hissed and began to wrap the guardian with his accusation-laced appendages, the only weapon he had.

Enoch pulled the demon's face close to his own.

Then with an act that shocked Dezro, the normally docile guardian let out a warrior cry that had been kindled in the depths of his being. The intense cry evaporated the fight right out of the demon.

Dezro became a quivering heap of rot.

As he whimpered, powerless in the face of the guardian, Enoch pulled the demon yet closer and whispered into his ear,

"You are finished."

As the words sounded in Dezro's ear, the demon jolted in pain as the guardian's sword thrust into his chest cavity. Enoch tightened his grip around the demon's neck and the decomposed shell exploded into ash and was carried away to the lake of fire, the fallen leader's final destiny.

Emergency Room

"Pay attention to the road. I've got to find this hospital," Scott said to himself as the demonic accusations ceased. "Babe, are you still with me?"

"Ah, ha," she quietly replied.

"We're almost there, Hon," he reassured his precious bride.

"There it is! Thank God."

He took the final curve, Munson Hospital's main entrance; the lighted sign beamed like a lighthouse in the dark night sky.

Scott swung into the main entrance on a mission to find the emergency room.

Following the driveway as it curved through a grove of evergreens, Scott saw the sign he was looking for. "Emergency Entrance. Got it!"

He pulled the truck under the canopy and jumped out shoeless and still in his swimming trunks.

As Scott circled around to the passenger's side, a nurse met him on her way out of the Emergency Room doors.

"We had a diving accident! My wife stopped breathing. I had to resuscitate her," he said with a quiver still in his voice.

"Is it a decompression injury then?" the nurse asked.

"I don't think so", he replied. But really, it sounded more like a question, because he hoped *she* could tell *him* that answer for sure.

The nurse grabbed a nearby wheelchair, got Darnisha out of the truck, and wheeled her into the check-in area.

Scott jumped back into the truck and headed for the parking lot, pulling into the nearest spot.

He grabbed his shoes and a pair of pants out of the truck and threw them on as he hurried into the emergency entrance.

The admitting nurse directed him back to the room where they had already taken Darnisha.

As Scott entered the room, he found several doctors already checking her out.

"Hi, Mrs. Taylor. Can you tell us your name? Do you know where you are? Are you able to speak?"

She replied in a weak but stable voice, "Yes, my name is Darnisha. My husband and I are here for the weekend."

"Thank God. She's talking with the doctor," Scott breathed a sigh of relief.

"Let's get some tests going right away," the doctor instructed the nurse as he exited the room.

The nurse turned towards Scott and handed him a clip board with a quarter inch of papers attached.

"Hello, Mr. Taylor. Can you fill out these forms for me?" We will be back shortly to take your wife for some tests."

"Ok, sure, thank you, " Scott replied unengagingly, his focus still on his wife.

Scott sat beside Darnisha's gurney and started going through the stack of forms.

As Scott struggled to think clearly enough to answer the list of questions, Israfel entered the room and inspired Darnisha to reach over and grab her husband's hand.

Scott paused and looked up from the forms and towards his wife as she began to speak.

"Baby, you're my hero."

Scott could barely grin, but shook his head still feeling so much guilt over what had happened to her.

"I don't feel like a hero," he replied.

"In fact, I don't feel much of anything," still numb from the ordeal.

To Darnisha, he had given her a new life; a life where she was never a single woman.

She would always be a part of him and she was forever grateful.

"I love you, Hon," she said quietly.

"I love you, too."

Connected in spirit just a handful of days ago, tonight they were connected in soul.

Scott had breathed life into a woman who was always and forever to be his wife and he would forever and always be her husband.

As he felt his emotions welling up inside, he excused himself from the room. "I'll go get you some dry clothes to change into. I'll be just a minute."

"OK Baby, please hurry back."

The bewildered husband, walked as if in a trance out of the emergency room to the parking lot and truck.

His exit was not for the clothes but the need to reach out to someone before he totally lost control of his emotions.

"Who do I call? God, I have to talk with someone. I need somebody to pray."

He slipped his cell phone out of his pocket, opened it to his contact list, and scrolled down to "Mom and Dad."

With hands still shaking, he pressed the send button and lifted the phone to his ear.

It started to ring as he cleared his throat and prepared to give his best sounding *"everything is all right"* voice.

The ringing stopped and Scott heard his younger brother's voice, "Hello?"

"Hey man," Scott responded as upbeat as he could

"Is mom or dad around?"

His brother caught the unusual quiver in Scott's voice and with concern asked, "What's going on?"

"Ah, we had a bit of an accident."

"What? What kind of an accident?"

"Well, a diving accident. But everything is all right."

"What happened?"

"Ah, well, Darnisha and I got separated and…Darnisha drowned."

"Oh my God!"

"She's doing fine. I found her in time and she's fine."

"So, she's all right?"

"Yeah, she's in the emergency room right now getting checked out. They are doing x-rays and a brain scan and checking her lungs and heart and to make sure there is no damage."

"Thank God."

That was the first time in a long time Scott had even heard his brother utter the name of God in a positive sense.

"Yes, definitely. Well, I've got to get back in there. Can you tell Mom and Dad what happened and ask them to pray for us?"

"No problem. Are you ok?"

"Yeah. I'm just kind of shaken up right now. Anyway, tell them I will call again later."

"O.k., take care, man." Scott's brother said, understandably concerned.

"I will. Talk to you later."

Scott turned his attention back to the truck and rummaged through the wet dive equipment to find Darnisha's things.

He stopped for a moment, put his head down on the floor of the truck, and started to cry. Like a reflex, he jerked his head up and wiped the tears away.

"This isn't over. I still have to be strong for Darnisha," he coached himself.

He grabbed her dry clothes and shoes, shut the truck and returned to the emergency room.

He walked through the maze of hallways to her room.

As he walked in the room, he nearly tripped on the telephone cord that was stretched across the room and behind the curtain that surrounded Darnisha's bed.

Scott pulled back the curtain and was surprised by the sight of his wife on the phone.

"I love you too, Mom, good-bye," Darnisha said.

"Was that my mom?! I just called them. How did they know where we were? I never told them." Scott was dumbfounded. Five minutes hadn't even passed since he had spoken with his brother.

"You know mamas always know, Baby," Darnisha joked.

"You're right! How do they do that?" they both chuckled at the thought.

In fact, his mother's guardian had spoken a word of knowledge into her panic-stricken spirit and had given her direction of where to find them.

Scott sat numb next to Darnisha's gurney in the E.R.

She reached over and grabbed his hand and squeezed.

"You saved my life, Baby," she said softly.

Tears welled up in his eyes. He smiled at her.

"What happened, Baby?" Scott asked, still desperate to know what went wrong.

Darnisha slowly began to attempt to recount all the details of her ordeal.

As she finished recalling the best she could, the doctor entered the room with a smile on his face.

"Well, I have the results of the blood test, x-rays and E.K.G. And I'm glad to report that everything looks great," he said confidently.

"There is no sign of any brain damage, lung damage, or heart irregularities. I still would like to keep you overnight to make sure that there are no complications or residual problems."

"No, I don't want to stay," Darnisha protested.

The doctor responded, "Well, if your husband is willing to stay up and watch you, I will consider letting you go. You see, once the body has suffered this kind of trauma, you could stop breathing or your heart could stop again. So it will be very important to keep an eye on you for the next 24 hours."

Scott replied, "No problem."

"Are you sure that's ok, Babe? I don't want to stay here."

"Yeah, Babe, I don't think I can sleep anyway."

"Ok. Well, if you have any questions or concerns throughout the night bring her back in right away," said the physician.

"Okay, I will. Thank you, Doctor," Scott said as he shook the doctor's hand vigorously.

In the hospital's parking lot, Scott pulled the truck up under the breezeway just as the nurse was rolling Darnisha out of the doors.

He jumped out to help lift her in. He opened the door and the nurse walked to the side of the wheelchair to assist Darnisha into the truck. Before the nurse could help, Darnisha stood up and climbed into the truck on her own. Scott felt another layer of his protective guard drop as he watched.

In the spiritual realm, all the hosts of heaven involved in the Taylor's deathgate began to celebrate as they usually do after a successful gateway transition.

The atmosphere was charged with excitement. "Praise to the Almighty Merciful God" filled the air. The heavenly hosts danced as joyful music echoed throughout the realm of glory.

The guardians laughed and shared dreams and hopes for the couple's future. They were each so proud of the Taylor's for making it through.

All the guardians could sense the immense responsibility lift. All, that is, except Enoch.

Enoch, Scott's guardian, sat off by himself deep in thought and intercession.

Israfel, noticed him alone and removed from the celebration.

She nudged her way through the crowd of dancing angels over to the pensive Enoch.

"Why aren't you celebrating for your Scott?"

Enoch, drawn out of his trance by the question, looked at Israfel with a smile that quickly faded leaving only deep concern for Scott over his face.

"I sense it is not over for us; this is going to be hard for Scott to recover from.

I must be vigilant and keep watch.

The enemy is not done with him.

Scott has many more battles coming soon. He will need strength beyond me to make it through."

Darnisha's Secret Place

As Darnisha climbed into the truck, mentally she climbed into her secret place of serenity and self-protection.

This place was created when she was only five years old.

It was a place she had created to isolate from the turmoil she faced attempting to cope with an emotionally abandoned family life.

Darnisha was conceived out of wedlock by her parents, high school sweethearts at the time.

Because of the times, and pressure from family, the couple quickly married.

They soon found their new relationship strained and frustrating. The newly added life they were now responsible for made the patched together union emotionally stunted.

Before the couple could evaluate and work through the new relationship, Darnisha's mother was diagnosed with multiple sclerosis, was completely bed ridden, and not expected to live.

Darnisha's father, overwhelmed with many things in his young life and the unexpected illness of his wife, chose to detach and pull away.

At five years old, Darnisha was responsible for the unreal, unnatural, unfair expectation of caring for her sickly mother and infant baby brother.

Unbelievably, she made a decision most adults could not make. She decided that her feelings, emotions, and problems were not important. The wellbeing of her mother and brother became her priority.

She needed to be strong for them, to take care of their daily needs, something her mother was unable to do and her father chose not to.

Darnisha, at that moment, traded in her toy baby dolls for the daily demanding care of her baby brother.

She traded in a child's request for an afternoon treat for cooking dinner for her bedridden mother.

To compensate for this dysfunctional decision, Darnisha's mind began constructing a fortress of solitude.

The fortress became the place she would run to. It also became the burial ground for all her fledgling emotions, fears, anger, loneliness, and depression.

Over the decades to follow Darnisha continued to reinforce the walls of the Fortress and pack unresolved emotions under the now-bulging floorboards.

Sitting in the front seat of the couple's SUV, she ran back to her familiar comforting fortress.

Unwilling and unable to handle, or even begin to process, what had happened or could have happened to her that day.

As she mentally sat in her accustomed safe place, unknowingly to her, the bricks and mortar of her fortified fortress began to crack and pull apart slowly, by divine appointment. This would be the beginning of the end of her self-inflicted fortress, which was in fact a life-muting prison.

But for now she was safe, and that is all that mattered to her.

Sleepless Night

Scott had stayed many nights in Traverse City over the years. There was only one place he could imagine being after an ordeal like this one.

He headed towards the East Bay and to a small resort he had frequented many times. This place felt like home to him with its comfortable rooms and beautiful view of the East Bay.

It had the coziness of home and they both needed that tonight.

Darnisha was still weak and barely able to sit up. So he stopped at a drug store to pick up some juice and snacks for her.

Just down the road, he could see the pink and gray-lighted sign for Points North hotel.

"We're almost there, Babe."

As they got closer, Scott could see the words "No Vacancy" glowing in red.

"Oh, no. God, please let them have a room for us," he quietly whispered. A sense of panic came over him.

He wasn't in a state of mind to search from hotel to hotel to find a place to stay. He wanted to stay in a place that was comforting and he could settle his mind and emotions.

Scott had no indication that there was a room set aside and waiting for them. One picked out by his faithful guardian who had caused it to be overlooked by management before they turned the "No Vacancy" sign on.

He pulled into the parking lot and up to the main lobby anyway. As Darnisha rested in the passengers seat, he sat there for a moment and started to feel overwhelmed. His emotions pushed to the surface.

"God, help me, please." After his short prayer, he decided to check and see if they had any rooms. He slowly stepped out of the truck, feeling light-headed, and walked into the hotel office.

An older, attractive woman was behind the desk. She was cleaning up for the night. Scott cleared his throat and said, "Hello," very softly, "Is there any chance that you might have a room available for this evening?"

She made a grimacing face of disapproval and went to the computer. After a few keystrokes and double-checking, her face changed to perplexed. She said, "Wow, ok, it seems we have a king-size room. Would that be alright for you?"

"Any room would be fine but a king-size would be great!"

"Well, somehow this room got overlooked in our booking this evening, so you are in luck," The woman replied.

"That would be absolutely wonderful." Scott was so relieved and had no idea that this was divinely planned, without one smidgin of luck to do with it.

"Enjoy your stay," the woman said politely as Scott turned to exit with the keys.

He walked out of the office into the cool night air and glanced upward, "Thank you."

As he slid back into the truck, he reassured his bride, "We got a room here, Baby."

"Great, Baby," Darnisha whispered back half asleep.

Scott then pulled the truck into the nearest parking space and helped her out and up the steps to their room.

He fumbled to unlock the door to the second floor room. It was the same as he remembered, pastel striped wallpaper with coordinating original artwork, a small kitchen area, a large Jacuzzi tub and a glass sliding door to a balcony overlooking the beautiful bay.

"This place feels like home to me. I certainly needed this!" Scott said to his barely conscious wife.

He put his sweetheart to bed and clicked on the TV to keep her company while he took care of a few things.

"Babe, I am going to get our bags. Will you be all right for a minute?"

"I think so, but please hurry back."

"Ok, Babe," he replied as he exited the room.

Scott hadn't brought the bags up on purpose because he really needed a minute away to gather his thoughts. He did not want to worry her but he really needed to talk to someone.

It was all so surreal.

He still hadn't processed all that had happened. Finally, he could feel the shock waves. He felt so alone. He needed to hear a comforting voice.

Scott had not realized that he was under such spiritual tension.

"Call your pastor," Enoch gently prodded.

Scott thought of his pastor and friend, now living in Sacramento, where he was planting a new church.

He grabbed his cell phone and anxiously scrolled through the numbers. Upon finding it, he hit Send and nervously cleared his throat. As he did he felt his emotions bubbling up.

After a few rings, he heard a click and the sound of a crowd yelling and shouting. Then a familiar voice, "Hello, this is Pastor Hagan."

"Hello, Pastor," Scott held back the tears and replied, "This sounds like a bad time for you."

"No! It's ok. I'm just at my son's football game."

Scott had never met anyone who loved watching his sons play sports more than his pastor.

"No, Pastor, I can call back."

"No, Scott, it's all right. What do you need?"

Over the sounds of the crowd cheering, Pastor Hagan could hear the cracking in Scott's voice that wasn't normally there.

Scott began to tell him what had happened. As the words came streaming out, so did his tears.

As he recounted the story to his pastor, Scott heard nothing but the sound of the crowd on the other end of the line. "Hello? Pastor Hagan? Are you still there?" Scott asked, thinking that maybe they had lost signal.

Finally, Pastor Hagan spoke, "Scott, oh my Lord. I don't know what to say! I can't believe that just happened. I'm sorry. I'm just shocked. How did you give Darnisha CPR in the water?!"

"I don't know, Pastor. I just really feel that this was all my fault."

"That's crazy. You are a hero! You saved her life!"

Scott broke down and began to cry.

"Let me pray with you right now."

Pastor Hagan prayed a prayer of thanksgiving, encouragement, and healing for the couple.

The Holy Spirit moved quietly into the moment and blanketed Scott with a soothing calm.

"Amen."

"Scott, I love you, man. Make sure you get some rest and take care of yourself and Darnisha. Just remember, you are her hero, Buddy.

Let me know how you're both doing. Call anytime, OK?!"

Scott promised to keep in contact and they said their good-byes. With this, he composed himself and headed back up to the room.

He entered the room to find his new bride fast asleep. Scott then walked over to the TV, turned it down, grabbed the bag of chips and sat up in bed beside her.

As he watched his wife's body rise and fall with each breath, he realized how something so uneventful that he had taken for granted was now so miraculous and comforting.

In the months to come, Scott would do this every time he woke up…watch her breathe.

The night seemed to drag on.

Darnisha slept soundly through the night without any problems.

She finally woke up and behaved like it was any other morning.

"Honey, what do you want to do today? I was thinking about going kayaking," She said in a chipper voice.

Scott looked at her like she was speaking a different language.

"Did I just have a nightmare?" he thought.

"Did last night really happen or was it all just a dream?"

Scott asked, "Baby, are you ok? How are you so ready to go right now?"

"I know it was a crazy day, but I don't want it to ruin our whole trip," she responded with enthusiasm that disturbed him.

He didn't realize she was still in shock.

He immediately felt the strange sensation again of being alone. Like he had just experienced this horrible crisis by himself.

He couldn't hold it together anymore. He broke down and began to weep. His massive frame trembled like a leaf.

All the emotions he was holding back came flowing out like the tide.

"I'm sorry, Hon. I want to be strong, but yesterday was so horrible. I can't possibly think about going back on the water," Scott blurted out over the tears.

After several emotional moments, he regained his composure and said, "Babe, you're not allowed to do any more water activities. I'm even thinking that means no baths at this point." They both chuckled. A much needed break from the intensity.

He stood up and put his arms around her. The frazzled couple held each other for a while.

He enjoyed the feeling of her breathing in his arms.

SCOTT ANTHONY TAYLOR   161

The End of Dezro

The defeated legion stood humbly before Lucifer, awaiting judgment.

"We have failed, my lord," were the only words to quietly emerge from head bowed injured remnants of the once proud regiment.

"Where is Dezro?"

"He did not make it, my lord."

"Ah, well I guess this battle was not all bad," the dark lord remarked sarcastically.

"We are not defeated. If we cannot take their lives, we can still tear them apart. I can make them abandon their covenant to God and each other and destroy their future together," schemed the evil master.

"How is that possible, my lord? The opportunity has passed."

"No," Lucifer barked.

"There is another way," he seethed. "There is still time to alter their path. I don't need you for this," he waved away the pitiful squad.

"This attack will be in my most successful arena. My specialty…
the mind," he rubbed his hands together like a villain with the
ultimate plan. "Oh, how I love playing with emotions," the
wicked lord began to salivate at the thought. "Watch and learn,
you imbeciles. I have not lost yet!"

The Morning After

"Wake up," Shemael, Patrick's guardian, whispered into his ear. It was early the morning after he had rescued the stranded divers. "Go back to the lake and find all of it," Shemael softly prompted.

"Hmmm. I think I'll go investigate where we found those two. See what we can find," Patrick said to himself.

Slowly, and as quietly as possible, he rolled out of bed so as not to waken his "non-morning-person" wife.

He picked up his shorts and shirt off the floor where he had dropped them the night before.

He crept slowly across the old wood floor attempting not to make any noise. He picked up his keys from the dresser, headed across the room, and opened the bedroom door.

The door creaked as it opened. Trixie was lying in her bed in the far corner and awoke at the sound.

When she was satisfied that it was her master and not an intruder, she relaxed, rested her head on her worn bed and drifted back to sleep.

Patrick continued out of the room and shut the door.

He walked softly down the stairs, through the kitchen, and out the back door.

He jumped into his truck and stuck his keys into the ignition. As he did he hesitated,

"This is kind of crazy," he said to himself. "What am I thinking? I'm not going to find anything."

"Just go take a look." The hope placed in his heart by the guardian was too great to resist.

"Ah, I'll just go take a look. It can't hurt." Patrick turned the key, put the truck into gear and headed to his boat.

As he pulled up to the dock, he gazed across the lake. A beautiful cloudless sky and below it, the stunningly clear water that Crystal Lake was known for.

The lake was as flat as a pane of glass with no signs of rough waters or wind.

"Boy, this sure is different from last night," Patrick noted aloud to himself.

He walked down the old wooden dock to his covered boat. He knelt down next to it, reached out and began to remove the canvas cover. He methodically folded it, stepped into the boat, and placed it onto the floor.

With a slight groan, Patrick stood up and unfastened the ropes from the cleats. With a push off the dock and a twist of the key, he was off.

As he turned the boat westward, he took a deep breath of the clean morning air.

He reached over to the throttle controller.

"Well, let's see what we can find." He felt an odd confidence as he nudged the throttle forward.

The engine awoke with a roar from its soft idle. The boat launched forward and up onto the surface of the water.

He steered the small vessel westward towards the site where they found Scott and Darnisha. He could feel the warmth of the rising sun on the back of his neck.

It reminded him of why he and Jacqueline had chosen to live on this lake. The tranquil balance of nature at the beginning of a new day was unmatched anywhere.

He carefully navigated the boat towards the northern coast of the lake where they had picked up the two less than 24 hours earlier.

As Patrick piloted his boat closer to the spot, he felt it. "Slow down and check here," Shemael whispered as he led him to the exact spot.

Patrick quickly slowed his boat and began to survey the surroundings.

"This is it," he said aloud as if he knew someone were there with him.

He shut off the engine and the boat drifted to a stop. He glanced over to the depth gage and saw the large digital readout flash "50 feet." He then looked overboard into the crystal water. From here he could see the tan sand and small green patches of grass on the lake bottom.

"Unbelievable," he said with a chuckle. "How could it have been so bad yesterday and so clear today?"

"Look over there," Shemael prompted.

Patrick began to scan the bottom. After several minutes, he saw something blue in color off to the left. He moved to the open bow of his boat and leaned over the edge.

"There is definitely something there. Let's see, how can I nab it?"

He grabbed the boat's anchor. "This should do it."

He slowly lowered it into the water and over the blue object resting on the lake bottom. Hand-over-hand Patrick lowered the anchor rope until the weight on the rope released.

"There, that's the bottom."

Very slowly, Patrick began to drag the anchor rope along the side of the boat. Suddenly, he could feel resistance on the anchor.

"Gotcha!"

He pulled a little harder on the line and it didn't budge. Then with his entire weight, he pulled again. The anchor began to rise off the bottom, but was ten times heavier.

"Ha! I got it!" Patrick said with belabored breath as he worked to retrieve his catch.

With all the strength the thin man could muster, he pulled foot-after-foot of the line aboard his boat.

As the anchor emerged from the depths, he could see the top of the object. Six more pulls on the line and the equipment faded into clear view.

"Yes! "

His speed quickened with excitement. Finally, his catch broke the lake surface and there it was: a blue scuba BC, a dark blue air tank still attached to a regulator, and pressure gauges.

"Well, look at that," Patrick could not help but smile.

He removed the anchor from the BC and swung the scuba tank around to grab it with his other hand. As he did, he noticed something clear hanging around the chrome attachment at the top of the tank.

He quickly reached to grab it before it dislodged. "And the mask too! I never thought I'd find this."

He wrestled the waterlogged equipment onto the edge of his boat and rolled it onto the seat cushion.

He stood and exclaimed, "Woo! That baby is heavy!"

Catching his breath, he knelt down to examine the gear. "Man, they are not going to believe this," he chuckled with a feeling of great accomplishment. "Wait till they see this!"

"Wow, these kids must really have heaven lookin' out for them," Patrick said.

Just then the guardian quoted the words Jesus had spoken over the deathgate, "…and nothing will be lost."

Besame Mucho

The shock of the event had left them both feeling numb. They packed the truck and checked out of the hotel. Darnisha was very hungry so they decided to head downtown to one of their favorite restaurants in Traverse City.

It was a quiet ride.

Scott really didn't know what to say.

He could not possibly articulate the multitude of thoughts and intensity of his feelings in the fifteen-minute drive anyway.

They parked and walked around to the front of the restaurant where the hostess was standing. She led them through the front door and out to a quaint covered patio.

The couple sat down next to each other as the hostess rattled off the day's specials.

"Welcome, you two. We have..." Neither of them paid much attention to the bubbly young girl.

Scott's first intention was to find a stiff drink on the menu to help his frazzled nerves. The hostess took the order and left the couple alone for a few moments.

Darnisha did not mind Scott's order.

"That sounds kinda good right now, huh? What a day." Although it was rare for Scott to order a drink, Darnisha usually had something negative to say or at least gave him a disapproving look.

But a cocktail today did not seemed to be that big of a deal anymore. In fact, it seems like exactly the right time for it.

Another waitress greeted them, "Here's your order, sir." She sat a beautiful martini glass in front of him filled with cool clear liquid and a large green olive lying on the bottom. She took their food order while Scott took a large swallow.

"Ah," he let out a quiet sigh as the warmth of the liquid passed down his throat. He relaxed in his seat and took a deep breath. They both watched the end-of-summer shoppers perusing the quaint galleries and specialty shops that lined old Main Street.

Aneal, the archangel of passion, was on assignment from God to help the couple overcome their shock and to bring encouragement for the two to lean on each other for strength.

Knowing that both were romantics at heart, she guided the restaurateurs' music selection.

"Ah, here's a great mix," the restaurant owner said as he flipped through his collection of CD's. Just then, the beautiful melody floated across the restaurant to Scott and Darnisha's table. As they listened, it instantly brought both of them to tears.

"Besame, besame, mucho…" Diane Krall sang it so well.

It was one of the couple's favorite songs. The message and her voice melted their anxiety in that moment and brought their gaze to one another.

Scott tearfully looked over at Darnisha as her tears welled up and flowed down her cheeks. He reached out and grabbed her hand and they wept together.

The waitress didn't know what to think as she brought out the couples' entrées to the table and saw them both crying. "Are you all ok?" she asked feeling a bit awkward about invading this personal moment.

Scott quickly wiped the tears from his eyes and gave her a smile, "We're all right. Thank you."

"Well, let me know if you need anything else," she offered as she left their table.

"Thank you."

"Babe, things will never be the same, will they?" Darnisha asked what they were both thinking.

Pat and Jackie

The couple left the restaurant and headed towards the western coast.

"I can't believe you just dropped all that gear on the bottom of the lake. Wow! You do love me," Darnisha joked.

"Yeah. I'm sure it's long gone," Scott surmised.

Just then he glanced at his phone and noticed there was a message.

"Jacqueline just called me!"

"I want you to meet these folks, Hon. I need to thank them."

"Sure, I need to thank them, too," Scott replied.

"She invited us to come to their home. She said they have a surprise. I wonder what it is?"

"Let's go find out," Darnisha encouraged.

It was a beautiful day. The sky was blue and the sun rays warmed the air to just the right temperature.

The drive was relaxing and enjoyable, just what the exhausted couple needed.

After a pleasant 40-minute drive Scott and Darnisha pulled into the quaint town of Beulah again.

Soon after entering the small town, they pulled into Patrick and Jacqueline's driveway.

Crystal Lake could be seen from the front yard.

The couple walked across the yard and knocked on the front door.

Immediately an energetic bark began pulsing inside the home. A woman's voice could be heard behind the door shouting, "Trixie! Get away from the door!"

Slowly the door opened in spite of Trixie against it. Soon it was open enough for the couple to see the smiling face of Jacqueline.

It was like seeing beloved long lost relatives.

"Come on in and make yourselves comfortable!" Jacqueline excitedly proclaimed as she grabbed both of them and gave them a huge hug.

Scott and Darnisha made their way into the house, giving attention to the excited Trixie.

"Patrick, they're here! Get down here!"

In a moment, Patrick appeared coming down the stairs heading to the family room.

"This is Patrick, my husband. Honey, you remember this couple don't you?"

"I sure do", Patrick responded as he stuck his hand out towards Scott.

"You guys look much better than you did yesterday."

SCOTT ANTHONY TAYLOR   173

Scott smiled and grabbed Patrick's hand firmly with gratitude.

"Patrick, this is my wife, Darnisha. I don't think you guys officially met."

Scott released Patrick's hand so he could offer it to Darnisha. Immediately Darnisha pushed past it with her body as she grabbed Patrick with a giant hug.

"It is great to meet you, thank you!" Darnisha said as she continued to embrace him.

"Come on in and sit down," Jacqueline continued.

Darnisha let go of Patrick and found a spot on the sofa in the living room next to her husband.

Jacqueline, who clearly was the talker in the family said,

"It is so good to see you both. What an ordeal yesterday, huh? How are you doing today, sweetheart?"

"We're doing ok. Much better than when you saw us yesterday. I really didn't get to talk to you much when we met but I really wanted to thank you for helping us," Darnisha responded.

"Oh, no problem, Dear. You were not looking very well. You look like a totally different person today!"

"Yeah, you clean up real well, young lady," Patrick joked. They all laughed at the lighthearted comment.

"Well, thank you both very much for everything you did. We are forever grateful," Darnisha said again as Scott chimed in with her this time.

"You guys really affected our lives too," Jacqueline continued. "We told our neighbors and some friends what happened and we really wanted to share with you guys how we ended up on that side of the lake."

Jacqueline began telling Scott and Darnisha the story of how their day had gone and how miraculous it was that they found them at all.

"We never go to that side of the lake because is so far for us," Jacqueline said. She continued now more seriously, "I truly believe that God ordained our steps to be on the lake at that spot and at that time just for you."

"Amen, we believe that too", Scott responded.

Patrick piped up, "Hey, come out to my truck. I have something for you."

They walked out the side door of the house to the Blazer. Patrick walked to the back and opened the doors. There sat Darnisha's entire scuba gear set: everything, including her silicone facemask. For a moment they were speechless. "What in the..."

When Scott was able to speak, he asked, "How in the world did you get this?"

"Well, I went back this morning to the spot where we found you and I could see the gear sitting on the bottom of the lake. I took the boat anchor, threw it down and hooked the equipment, then pulled it to the surface," Patrick joyfully responded.

"Unbelievable!! That is amazing!" Scott said with tears in his eyes.

"How can we ever thank you both?" Darnisha choked out trying to hold back her tears.

"Don't even worry about it," Jacqueline responded with a big smile across her face.

Patrick helped Scott transfer the gear to the back of the Yukon. The couples said their good-byes with hugs and teary eyes. They all promised that they would keep in touch.

"We will never forget you two."

"We feel the same. God bless you both. Drive carefully."

Scott and Darnisha pulled out of the driveway, waved good-bye, and headed to the interstate. As they drove home, Scott had a sudden revelation.

"Look at that, Baby, we didn't lose one piece of equipment," Scott said.

"Wow! God is good isn't He, Honey," Darnisha replied. "Thank you, Lord."

Heading Home

The usual relaxing drive home and good conversation gave way to a silent three-hour ride.

Darnisha drifted off into much needed sleep. Scott drifted too, but into his automatic driver mode, eyes fixed on the road ahead.

"This looks like a good time to begin," Lucifer chided as he planted his first haunting image in Scott's mind.

As Scott focused on the white lines, the image of his wife's lifeless face overtook his thoughts and began to consume him. He felt like he had just grabbed a live electrical wire. He tried to push the image out of his mind as he adjusted himself in his seat.

"Uh, focus, Scott. Everything is fine," he coached himself.

He took a deep breath and looked over at his sleeping wife to make sure she was still breathing. Seeing the reassuring movement of her chest raise then sink again, he focused his attention back to the paging of the white lines. This exercise continued a good dozen or more times until they finally reached their neighborhood.

He pulled into the circle driveway and shut off the engine.

"Home, thank God," he thought.

He took another deep breath and gently shook Darnisha to wake her.

She awoke with a jerk and glassy eyes trying to get her bearings.

"We're home, Babe".

"Ok."

It was dark and well past 10 PM. Scott was very tired and ready for his own bed. Darnisha was still half asleep doing the minimum she needed to get into bed and back to sleep.

Scott quickly unloaded the truck and headed to the room. They both breathed a sigh of relief when they saw their comfy bed. They each felt very blessed to live in such a beautiful house. They had just moved all of their furniture in a few weeks before and it was just starting to feel like home.

Tonight, it especially felt like it.

They changed their clothes and crawled under the blankets. Everything felt more comforting and cozy than before.

"Wow," Scott said, "I would never have guessed that everything we just went through could have happened since the last time I was in this bed."

As they lay there looking up at the ceiling, he heard Darnisha sniffle.

He turned to her and saw tears coming down her face. The small stream became heavy weeping and within moments the weeping turned into whaling and shaking.

The shock was finally wearing off and the reality of what happened hit her all at once.

He reached over and put his arms around her quivering body.

"It's OK, Baby. Everything is okay," Scott whispered over and over again in her ear as she cried herself to sleep.

"Comfort your bride now because a new gateway is before you, Scott," said Enoch as he hovered near the tired man embracing his sweetheart. "This gateway will test your faith and you will face your inner pain."

A new gateway appeared. This one didn't explode into existence as the deathgate had. It slowly crept from the darkest depths of hell where it was birthed. This one was long and twisted. This dark distorted gateway would take weeks, months to pass through. This one was for Scott.

Berakiel's Assignment Begins

The moon shone through the second floor leaded glass windows gently illuminating a spectacular mahogany paneled cavernous room. A shadow of a king sized 4-poster bed stretched across the parquet floor. Under the imported sheets lay an elderly man who began to toss and turn as Berakiel, the angel of worldly wisdom and favor, began troubling his sleep.

Finally, after several minutes of Berakiel's promptings, the man opened his eyes. He took a deep breath and with a slight groan, rolled over and sat up in bed.

With another deep breath, he stood up and slowly walked across the huge bedroom to an adjacent office library. The man walked towards a large elaborately carved desk sitting in front of a marble fireplace.

He pulled out the high back tufted leather chair and slowly lowered himself into it. He leaned forward to turn on his computer and started going through numerous unopened emails.

Berakiel again troubled the man's mind with boredom of his current activity. The guardian softly whispered encouraging thoughts to switch his attention to an Internet search engine.

While the man scrolled through his normal searches, Berakiel revealed a divinely appointed thought. The revelation hit the man who quickly responded by changing his Internet search. As he clicked through the information, he felt the familiar inspiration of a new business idea. He felt this many times in his life. Each inspiration seeded a multi-million dollar business. He was a very successful businessman based in Sacramento.

In fact, he was on the top 500 wealthiest businessmen in the world. He was a billionaire.

Now after dozens of business ventures, the eighty-year old entrepreneur was trying to retire. He thought the inspirations were done.

"I guess I still have some new ideas left in me," he chuckled to himself as he continued to search out more information on his new inspiration.

Act III
The Long Recovery

A lightning bolt flashed, briefly illuminating the dark stormy night sky. Sheets of pouring rain and treacherous white-caped waves began to overtake a fleet of small dive boats.

The storm came out of nowhere. No one expected it or was prepared for it.

Scott was one of the divers below the surface of the water when the storm hit.

He was trying to fight the sudden heavy currents to reach the boat's anchor line to follow back to the surface.

The dive had been going well until the water turned dark and the currents started pulling the divers back and forth. Scott finally found the anchor line and started his slow ascent to the surface.

He had no idea what awaited him.

Hand over hand he struggled his way to the surface.

The anchor line was pulling up and down, furiously jerking him like a rag doll. He figured if the line was rough, the surface was going to be even worse.

Sure enough, when he broke the surface he had come up into a foreboding thunderstorm.

The dive boat was being pummeled by the huge waves; the sky was black as night and swirling with ominous clouds.

As he fought the pounding waves to reach the boats rear platform, a dive master onboard one of the other dive boat's yelled out,

"Shark!"

Scott turned to his left and saw the large dorsal fin sticking a good foot and a half out of the water.

He quickly submerged to see what this fin belonged to. As he looked through the churning water, he could clearly see a monster great white circling the boat.

A shiver of terror shot through his body.

He immediately headed back to the surface where he continued to struggle against the waves to reach the stern of the boat and the dive ladder.

Finally reaching the dive ladder, with one hand he grabbed hold of one of the last rungs.

Scott was being flung up and down with the boat like a bobbing cork.

He tried to hold on but keep his distance so as not to get hit by the thrashing boat.

He felt near exhaustion from battling the waves; also the fear of the man-eating predator so near added to his fatigue. Still not able to get on the boat, he submerged again to escape the brutal pounding of the waves. Again Scott reached out for the bottom rung of the ladder.

Grabbing it with one hand, he swung himself around to see the great beast swimming directly towards him.

Exhausted, he fought to pull himself and all his gear up the ladder but he was no match for the speed of the ocean's most ferocious killing machine.

The shark's eyes rolled back into its head as it opened its enormous jaws lined with giant razor sharp teeth and lunged at Scott.

All he could do was to scream through his regulator, "NO!!!"

Scott awoke bolting straight up in bed.

He was drenched in a cold sweat and gasping. He felt like he couldn't breathe.

He reached over to Darnisha and put his hand on her side. He could feel her chest expand with air, then, exhale.

She was still breathing, now if he could just catch his breath.

It was a nightmare.

"Ah! I get such a kick when they do that. Our master is a genius," Lucifer's minion celebrated as he observed Scott's struggle.

Scott caught his breath and tried to calm down.

After awhile of tossing and turning, he drifted back to sleep. "Oh, I'm not done with you. Think about this," Lucifer's helper dropped another disturbing idea into his subconscious.

Scott found himself in another horrific dream.

He thrashed and groaned so much that he woke Darnisha from her sleep.

"Wake up, Hon. Are you ok?"

"Calm down. It's just a dream."

The nightmares had become a common thing now after the accident.

Night after night for weeks, the dreams continued, all with a similar theme.

Every night a new nightmare produced the same reaction.

The vision of Scott seeing his new bride dead haunted his thoughts.

Every time he closed his eyes, he saw her lifeless face and her empty glazed eyes staring at him. In fact, he was having a hard time looking at her in the face at all.

He could watch her breathe and loved to hear her talk, but he couldn't bring himself to look directly into her eyes.

"Your wife is alive, Scott. Get a grip," he scolded himself. Still he could not shake the shock the accident had on him.

Guilt was consuming him as he relived the dive over and over again in his mind. All he could see were mistakes he made and it made him angry with himself.

"I've been trained better than that," he kept telling himself. He had been trained for events like this, better than most.

In search of a scuba instructor, Scott found the best. In a small town along the Lake Michigan shoreline was the headquarters of a diving legend.

The man, with over 40,000 logged dives, had found countless shipwrecks throughout the Great Lakes. He did many of his dives in more than 500 feet of ice-cold water, alone.

This was the man Scott selected as his instructor. Safety was everything to the man and he had no problem failing an average of 50% of his students due to the fact they didn't understand the seriousness and dangers of scuba diving.

Now, Scott could only see the bad calls and wrong decisions made that could have prevented the accident.

The decisions haunted his mind causing him incredible anxiety.

Both Scott and Darnisha were suffering with anxiety attacks now.

This was Darnisha's greatest struggle. She had always been controlled and upbeat, but after the accident the anxiety made her as frail as a mouse for a while.

She could not function for long without Scott being close by.

One evening as they sat silently over dinner, Darnisha announced to Scott, "Babe, I think we need some counseling."

She knew he distrusted counselors more so than most men because of his past experiences.

But this time he was not defensive about getting help. "You're right, Babe. Let's talk with someone."

"I will call tomorrow and get us an appointment," she responded.

"OK."

Counsel

Two days later, they sat in the waiting room of a crisis counselor filling out what they thought was ridiculously detailed and irrelevant questions on more than a dozen pages. After thirty minutes of filling out forms they heard,

"The doctor will see you now." "Finally," Darnisha said rather sarcastically.

They followed the nurse along a series of hallways to an open door.

"Take a seat and make yourselves comfortable. The doctor will be in shortly."

Darnisha lead the way into the room as the nurse shut the door behind them. The room was a warmly decorated corner office with large windows looking out over the river that ran through the heart of downtown Grand Rapids.

They both took a seat on one of two matching sofas parallel to the large windows.

After a few moments a tall, slender, older gentleman opened the door slowly and took a step into the office.

"Hello, I am Doctor Richardson," the man said with a warm smile and an outstretched hand as he walked towards them.

"Hello, I'm Darnisha and this is my husband, Scott."

"Very pleased to meet you," he continued as he took a seat in a lounge chair, which sat opposite the sofa.

Dr. Richardson ran his hand through his thinning gray hair, adjusted his tie, and said, "Well, you two have been busy, haven't you?"

The couple chuckled as Scott responded, "Yes, we have had a full marriage after two months. I'm kind of nervous about what to expect next."

The nervous laughter told Dr. Richardson a lot about the fear the couple was facing.

"Well, why don't you tell me what has been happening? Let's go back a bit before the accident.

Tell me, how did you meet and marry?"

Darnisha and Scott began to explain how they met.

As they shared the details of their relationship, they became more at ease.

After a few moments of reminiscing, real smiles came to their faces as they interrupted each other correcting the other's interpretation of their love story. Then came the details of the most recent weeks.

The atmosphere became tense as they shared the struggles they both were facing. Through the couple's recollection of the events,

Dr. Richardson listened intently, writing many notes on the yellow legal pad.

As they concluded, Dr. Richardson looked up from finishing his notes, took a deep breath and said, "Wow, that was something. It is so rare for me to counsel a couple in a situation like this. To be able to hear both sides of the accident is very unusual for me.

Tell me, Darnisha, how have people been responding to you?"

"They have been incredibly supportive," she replied. "I work at a church so I get many emails, letters, and cards from friends and members."

"OK, good. How about you, Scott?" The doctor asked.

"Well, at first I was kind of a hero. But, the attention seemed to fade quickly, especially as I began to struggle and pull away from people," Scott responded.

"Hmm… interesting."

Dr. Richardson continued, "I feel I need to tell you about a friend of mine. He was in World War II and was a prisoner of war.

My friend told me that there was a lot of torturing for information in the prison camp. If the Nazi's wanted information from you, they would bring you and your closest friend into a room together.

The Nazi's would then ask you information. If you didn't tell them what they wanted to know, they would proceed to torture your friend.

You see, the Nazi's discovered that most soldiers could handle much more torture on themselves than they could handle watching their friend go through.

Darnisha, this trauma was harder on you physically because you actually died. However, the effect on Scott is far worse emotionally especially since he introduced you to his cherished hobby.

Scott, I'm sorry to say this but it is going to be a much longer road for you to get beyond." The doctor continued, "You are both battling with something that is called post traumatic stress disorder."

"We need to work with your medical doctor and get you some medication to help you through this time. As I said, each of you will deal with things differently.

But, our first order of business is to make sure you are both resting well."

The couple left the office feeling raw from revisiting the incident again. In spite of how unearthed they felt, they were grateful to be understood and getting help.

Bad Medicine

"Doctor, the symptoms aren't getting any better. In fact, I think they are getting worse. Is there something you can do?

I really need some relief of all this," Scott urged his medical doctor.

"Well, we must not have you on a high enough dosage. Let's double it," Doctor VanderKlok responded.

Scott added another pill to the one he took each morning.

"Please, let this help," Scott whispered to himself and to God.

In a week things got even worse.

"Babe, I'm starting to have chest pains," Scott complained. By this time, he was teetering on exhaustion because Darnisha could not function without him being everywhere she was…everywhere, including work.

If he was out of her sight for any length of time, she would have an anxiety attack.

Scott was still trying to be strong for her but he was running out of steam.

With all of the emotional and physical strain, soon the relationship was taxed.

Scott's frustration was being compounded because Darnisha was receiving a great deal of support from colleagues and congregates.

He felt left out and misunderstood.

With a combination of bad medicine and little support, he spiraled into depression.

He could not enjoy anything.

Life had become dull.

He felt a lack of purpose and meaning. His frayed emotions were now ruling his life.

One more time he contacted his doctor.

"It's still not getting any better, Doc

"Well, son, just double it again. You should feel better soon," the old doctor advised.

Scott added another pill to his morning regimen.

Two weeks later, Scott was now physically ill due to the lack of sleep and the multiple anxiety attacks he would battle everyday, while Darnisha was experiencing remarkable recovery.

Late one afternoon, she had gone into the office for a few hours and stopped into the grocery store on her way home.

"Hey, Babe," she said as she rushed to the dining table with her arms full of groceries.

"I need you to help me do a small group lesson for church starting next Tuesday night."

Scott felt something snap deep inside. It was as if every emotion was welling up simultaneously... anger, frustration, depression, hate, remorse, and fear bombarded his mind all at the same time. He couldn't contain it any longer. The diseased concoction began to pour out of him.

"I will not help you!

You do this to me all the time!

You never ask me first before you commit me.

I am sick of it!

I am sick of you!" Scott yelled till he could feel his skin becoming clammy and tears began to flow down his face.

"What the heck? Gees!" Darnisha responded sharply.

"Forget it, you don't have to do it. What is your problem?!"

Scott's chest began to tighten up.

It felt as if a semi truck just parked on it. He grabbed his head as the room started to spin.

He broke down and began to weep uncontrollably.

"I can't take it!," he screamed.

As he wept, he noticed that things began to get dark. The room seemed like it was getting far away.

Even Darnisha's voice grew distant.

He looked up at her, his eyes filled with fear and confusion and cried out, "I need help!"

Everything went black and like a sack of stones he fell to the floor.

"Scott, Scott! What is going on! Oh God, Oh No!,"

What seemed to Scott as a moment later, he slowly opened his eyes to bright lights and blurry figures looking down on him. Slowly the blurriness began to fade and there was Darnisha's smiling face leaning over him as she held his hand.

He was in a bed in a hospital room. "Hey, Baby."

He could tell she was relieved.

"How are you feeling, Honey?"

"I have felt better," he responded, trying to shake off the grogginess. "What happened?"

"You had a rare reaction to the medication. The medication you were taking has the opposite effect on your body. It was actually making you worse. They have taken you off it. The specialist feels very confident that there's another medication that will help you.

"I'm afraid to take anything else," Scott responded as tears began to fall down his cheek.

"I can't take this anymore. I feel like I am going crazy."

He was emotionally and physically worn out.

"Can they just give me something so I can sleep? I don't want to start any new medication yet."

"Okay, Babe. Don't worry, I'll take care of it," Darnisha responded and walked out to the nurse's station.

A few minutes later she was back, followed by a nurse holding a syringe.

"Hello, Mr. Taylor, how are we doing?" The nurse spoke in an upbeat tone.

"Tired," Scott responded.

"Well, you will be asleep very soon," the nurse assured him as she injected the syringe into the IV bag hanging alongside the bed.

"I'm sure you will feel much better tomorrow."

"I hope so."

The nurse smiled as she left the room.

"I can't do this anymore, honey," Scott whispered to Darnisha.

"This is not what I expected our life would be."

"Me neither," Darnisha responded with some sadness.

Scott closed his tear-filled eyes and softly prayed, "God, please help us. This is not what we signed up for."

Just then he drifted off to sleep as Darnisha put her head on his chest and began to cry.

Prayers to the Throne Room

Enoch entered the throne room of God bringing the prayer that Scott just prayed from his hospital bed.

Jesus immediately walked towards the guardian. As he did, Enoch knelt before him with his head hung low.

Jesus knelt down in front of Enoch and put his hand on his shoulder, "What is it, Enoch?"

"Scott is starting to crumble under the weight and constant bombardment. His mind is not handling this well, my Lord. His mind is falling into darkness.

The enemy is continuing to attack him by invading his sleep with nightmares and filling his days with self-doubt, guilt, and hopelessness.

The enemy has influenced the doctor. Scott is having adverse effects to the prescribed medications. They are making things worse by giving him great anxiety. He is weakening and thoughts of suicide linger longer each time the evil one delivers the suggestion."

Jesus, clearly distraught, turned towards the throne and with deep compassion and urgency in His voice cried out, "Father, please let me help your child!

Surely he has withstood enough.

Let me give him help in the area he doesn't have the ability to control. Let me heal his mind."

"I love him too, my Son.

He is special to me. But I have a plan.

No, my Son, you may not heal him.

Instead, give him and Darnisha confidence in this new medication. It will help his mind process this event."

"My Father, it breaks my heart to see his mind so stricken."

"It is not my will to heal him in this way.

For now, he needs this thorn in his flesh. If it is removed, he will lean on his own strength and not mine. I need to be his all."

"Thank you, my gracious Father."

Jesus turned back to Enoch,

"Go, give Scott confidence and hope in this new medication. Tell Israfel to give Darnisha the confidence and hope she needs to encourage him through this gateway."

"Thank you, my Lord." Enoch responded with a thankful heart, stood to his feet, bowed again,

and with a flash, faster than light he translated from the heavenly realm to Scott's bedside.

Opportunity Knocks

Everyone had left the office for the day, except for the elderly businessman. He was hard at work on his newly-inspired business idea.

Berakiel sprinkled some restlessness on the man causing him to get up from his desk and wander around his new office complex.

He had retired a year ago but hated it. So, he decided to open a small investment company just for something to do. The small company turned into a large organization employing dozens of people less than six months into the endeavor.

As he walked through the now empty corridors, Berakiel intervened again by passing a prompt into his thoughts.

" Go down and see if anyone is in the church office."

The man had graciously donated some of the office space in his building to a pastor who was starting a church in northern Sacramento.

The businessman walked into the offices and found that all the lights were dim except one coming from the senior pastor's office.

The elderly man followed the light to the office and found the church's pastor sitting behind his desk deep into his Bible study.

Out of the corner of the pastor's eye, he caught movement outside his door and looked up.

"Hello sir!, what are you doing here?"

"I didn't mean to bother you. I though I was the only one here this late," the businessman responded.

"No, Sir, I'm working late, too."

"Well, I don't want to bother your study." "Oh, no, come on in. I need a break."

The elderly businessman entered the office and took a seat.

"What are you working on now, Sir? What's your next great project?"

"Well, now that you mention it, I got a great idea for a new business. I found some interesting information on the Internet. It is going to be huge in California. In fact, it is going to be the wave of the future. It will change commercial construction forever."

"That sounds amazing," the pastor responded energetically.

"The only problem is, I can't seem to find someone to run the company for me."

"Really, that's funny I just received a resume' from a friend of mine from Michigan. He and his wife are trying to relocate to California. They feel God wants them to come out to help us plant this church."

"What's his background?"

"Well, he doesn't have any construction experience. But he was an executive vice president for a manufacturing company."

"Really?!"

"Yes, I got his resume' right here. I just printed it out.

Take a look."

The businessman reached over and grabbed the sheets of paper.

As he read through it, he began to feel excitement. Berakiel laid peace and confidence on the man's heart that he had found the man to start the company.

"Is this his current phone number?" the aged businessman asked, pointing to the top of the resume'.

"Yes, that is it."

With that and a slight groan, the businessman stood up as he continued reading the resume'.

"Hey, thanks Scott. I think I'm going to give him a call."

The man left the office and headed back across the complex towards his own.

As he did, he pulled out his cell phone and started dialing the number on the sheet.

A Strange Phone Call

It had been several weeks since Scott had been taking the new medication.

He started feeling like his old self. The panic attacks and anxiety had ceased and he was able to sleep again.

It was late afternoon as Scott drove Darnisha across town to the store. Pulling into the store parking lot, Scott heard the muffled sound of his cell phone ringing.

Fishing it out of his pocket, Scott looked at the number.

"916, I don't recognize that area code."

Usually, Scott let unknown phone numbers go to voice mail.

Enoch won't let him do that with this call. With Enoch's intense promptings, the next thing Scott knew, he hit the receive button and raised the phone to his ear.

"Hello?"

Yes, I have just read your resume'. I'm starting a new company in Sacramento. It is going to revolutionize the commercial construction industry in California and eventually the country.

Would you be interested in running it?

Scott's head immediately started to swim.

"Ah, Who is this?"

The man spoke his name and Scott's stomach filled with butterflies of excitement and nervousness. He knew that name. He had read about the incredible success of this man's life and professional career. As Scott stammered to find words, he eventually found the word "Yes".

After hearing that word, the man continued.

"I will have someone call you with some details. Why don't you and your wife come out and we can talk more?"

"That would be great," Scott responded.

"Great someone will be contacting you soon."

"Ok, thank you, Sir."

"All right"

The phone clicked.

Scott lowered his phone, stunned from what had just transpired in a handful of minutes.

"Baby, what's going on?" asked Darnisha.

She was confused by the shocked expression of her husband's face, as she listened to a strange mostly one-sided phone conversation.

Slowly Scott responded, "Babe, I think I was just offered a position running a new company in California."

"Wow, baby that's great… You think you have?"

A few weeks later, the couple was on a plane heading to Sacramento, the city where their pastor was planting a church in; God's divine plan.

Scott and Darnisha weren't traveling to their destiny alone. The couples' ever-faithful guardians accompanied them. Enoch and Israfel were so excited to see the couple through the altered direction of the deathgate, and the reward.

The couple was met at the airport by a chauffeur in a large custom black Escalade limo. The driver took Scott and Darnisha across the Capital City, to an exclusive neighborhood, and through a large gated driveway. At the end of the cabal stone drive was the breathtakingly beautiful city home of the successful businessman.

The couple walked up to the huge door and rang the doorbell.

An elderly gentleman opened the door.

"Hello sir, I am Scott and this is my wife, Darnisha."

As Scott introduced himself and his wife to the businessman, Barakiel, the man's stately guardian, smiled and bowed respectfully at Enoch and Israfel who where standing behind the couple.

The guardians had not seen each other since the initial book reading back in the great hall of the palace of God. The elder more experienced guardian, Barakiel, spoke.

"You have done well escorting your Children through a very tricky series of gates. You should be commended."

"Thank you, Barakiel, Enoch and Israfel responded with great honor.

"Ah, I have heard you have an amazing voice." The elderly man spoke with a smile to Darnisha. "Please come in. You are probably tired from your trip. Let me show you to the guesthouse."

Barakiel gave the businessman a familiar sense of confidence in his selection of the couple.

As the trio walked through the amazing home, Barakiel fanned a spark of generosity in the elderly man's heart. The couple's new host then reached for one of many sets of keys lying on a table.

"Here are the keys to my BMW. Use it until we get you a vehicle. It is in the fifth stall on the right."

The couple's host then led them across the immaculately manicured yard full of fountains and beautiful gardens, gardens that hosted parties for celebrities and dignitaries from around the world.

He then led the couple to a European villa style guesthouse just off to the side of the main house. The businessman told Scott and Darnisha to make themselves at home and bid them good night. As the businessman left the couple, Barakiel following the man, turned and spoke to Enoch and Israfel,

"Tomorrow morning, the gateway's prophecy will be completed."

He bowed again and Enoch and Israfel returned the same as he turned to escort the businessman to his room for the night

The next morning, Enoch awoke Scott early. Scott was very excited and nervous about the morning meeting. Enoch was just as excited as Scott, but not nervous for he knew the outcome of this day.

Scott dressed in a new suite and attempted to calm himself by preparing for the meeting he would soon face.

The black Escalade was waiting to take him to the corporate headquarters where the businessman's new board of directors waited to meet Scott.

He climbed into the Escalade limo. Enoch nurtured peace in Scott's heart on the short trip.

As Scott walked into the building, a pleasant receptionist escorted him into the boardroom. The businessman and six other businessmen, all millionaires, owners of other partnership businesses sat waiting. Behind the seated elderly businessman was Barakiel, standing vigilantly and stoically. Enoch nodded his head in respect as Barakiel did the same.

Scott took a seat and the elderly businessman immediately began to speak.

"We all read your resume. Do you think you can make this company successful?"

Enoch blew a spirit of confidence into Scott's heart and mind.

"Yes sir, I do."

"It will be hard work. It is a competitive industry."

"Yes sir, it is. I can do it."

Barakiel again nurtured the elderly man's heart with complete confidence in his decision.

"Well, if you want the job, it's yours. The sooner you can start, the better.

We will cover the expenses to relocate you out here.

You can stay at my house until we can get one built for you. Is your wife going to lead worship at the church?"

"Yes sir."

"Well, I'm sure the church doesn't have enough money to pay her yet. We will get her a part time job at one of our other companies. We'll make sure she's paid well.

All right, son let's see what you can do.

Make us some money."

"Yes sir, I will."

With that, the elderly businessman slowly got up along with the rest of the board and all shook Scott's hand.

In a complete daze, Scott said goodbye and headed back to the Escalade and back to what would be the couple's home for the next three months.

That was it. In a moment, all the weeks and months of praying for guidance and provision was completed.

206   SCOTT ANTHONY TAYLOR

Back on the Beach

"Scott! Scott!" Softly, just above the waves fading in and out with the wind, **Israfel** assisted the words of Darnisha to the ears of Scott.

Scott turned toward the voice and there was his wife, Darnisha sitting along the water's edge in a small cove surrounded by rocky cliffs.

"Honey, honey, come here. Look what I found! Come here! You have got to see this."

He smiled and began to walk towards her. As he put his head down as he turned again into the wind, he noticed the sand was replaced with small smooth multi-colored rocks.

As Scott kept walking, he noticed the rocks became even more colorful. Colors not normally associated with rocks. Emerald greens, mint green, navy blue, opal white, bright orange, and crystal clear. As he stepped to the ocean's edge, he peered into the water. Through the clear cold water could be seen the same colors become even more vibrant. It looked as if the ocean floor were made up entirely of precious gemstones.

"Absolutely beautiful," he whispered.

As Scott continued towards Darnisha he noticed off to his right, a narrow winding path wondering up the cliff. This path was an actual walking trail unlike the trail-turned-cliff-scaling Scott used.

"Great, where was that when I needed it." Scott thought to himself.

Where the path met the beach sat an elderly man next to a stretched out old tattered blanket.

Scott turned his steps towards the old man.

As he got closer, Scott could tell that the man was a local and had spent the majority of his life near the ocean.

His stringy hair had long since turned white with age along with his scruffy, scraggly beard. His skin was dark and leathery with long deep crevasses running across his forehead and more running from the edge of his noise down his concaved cheeks.

Scott was close enough now to see that there were things strung out across the worn blanket.

The items were all handmade jewelry with colorful rocks attached as focal pieces. There were necklaces, bracelets and earrings fashioned out of leather, twine, wire, and these curiously beautiful stones.

"Welcome to Glass Beach," the gravelly voice of the old man uttered with a smile.

"Glass Beach?" Scott asked.

"Yes, there is no other place on earth like it," replied the old man.

"How did this place come to be?" Asked Scott.

"Well, decades ago, the city use to dump all the trash and garbage into the ocean right here. After years of dumping, the environmentalists made a big enough fuss to finally get them to stop.

After many more years of the continuous crashing of the waves and the tides coming in and out, all the trash was washed away, and what remained deteriorated except for all the glass items. They just broke up and years of being tossed by the waves on the rocks polished them into beautiful gem-like stones. People come from all over to see and collect the beautiful gems."

Scott looked up from the collection of unique colorful jewelry and spotted Darnisha sitting on the beach filtering through the beautiful glass stones. Scott walked over to her and sat beside her on that rocky beach.

"This is amazing. Isn't it beautiful?" Darnisha said excitedly.

"Yes, you are," Scott thought to himself as he watched her child like excitement.

"Yes, Baby, this is incredible." Scott spoke softly. "It is crazy that all this beauty came from trash," Darnisha replied. Enoch, at his place right along Scott, reached over and touched his mind with divine enlightenment of the revelation of the beach and how it parabled the couples lives.

The analogy of the beach and the couple's lives hit Scott. What an amazing God to take something terrible and make it beautiful. Not just to fix it and restore it to its original beauty but to make it into a landmark phenomenon that draws more attention than it would ever have done before.

God did just that in the lives of Scott and Darnisha. From this potential tragedy and through the rocky rough recovery, God made them into something truly amazing.

Yes, Scott and Darnisha made it to California, for them, the land of milk and honey.

The couple's earthly dreams came true. They built their dream house, traveled the world, met world leaders and world changers. Scott even got Darnisha her dream car, a new baby blue Jaguar.

But much more importantly, in this land they found their passions and purpose and the supernatural provision to accomplish them.

Enoch and Israfel also sat on the beach alongside the couple.

"This is a beautiful place, for being in the physical realm, anyway." Israfel commented. "Yes, it is," Enoch agreed.

Not able to hold back her joy anymore Israfel shouted, "We made it!" and burst out into song. "Yes, we did." Enoch replied with a reserved smile.

"It has been good to see them laugh and enjoy life again," Enoch continued, trying to be heard over Israfel's singing.

"This new direction that our Lord is leading them is so exciting!" Israfel sang as she gracefully danced with the wind around Enoch.

"...also treturous. You do see the new gateway Almighty God is leading them to, don't you?" Enoch responded responsibly.

"Yes, I do, but our Lord says, let us not borrow from tomorrow's worries. Can we just enjoy this time today with them?" Israfel asked, smiling as she watched Scott and Darnisha picking through the rocks and laughing with each other.

Enoch releasing the thoughts of future battles turned and looked at the couple and smiled with a sense of accomplishment and pride.

"They made it," Enoch spoke softly before joining Israfel in songs of celebration.

God had provided for Scott and Darnisha time to rest, recover and enjoy his wonderful creations. Their relationship grew deeper together than they ever could have imagined.

God had given them a new focus and direction for their lives together. God challenged the couple to step out on faith and do what he had purposed them to do, something truly unique and exciting, but that is a different story and a new gateway...

A Final Thought to Ponder

I hope you enjoyed our story.

We hope you were able to grab hold of the many spiritual gems that were scattered like seeds along the way.

Seeds that if allowed to take root could grow into fruit in your life's adventure.

Indulge me to reiterate some important facts that you must realize in order to have any kind of peace and assurance in the seemingly chaotic events that make up our physical existence on this planet.

If you ever feel alone, abandoned, or isolated, don't.

All of heaven, the angels, the heavenly hosts, God the Father and his Son, all are focused on you, His child, on this minuscule marble of a planet.

They are all bent towards each of us. They lead and inspire us to find our purpose, walk in victory and finish well.

As a child of God, each of us has an entourage of angels, guardians, hosts, and ministering spirits all with an assignment from the beginning of time to protect, lift, minister, and fight not only for our lives but our very souls.

When you are in those times of great need, desperate times when you feel you are lost, alone, and can't make it, close your eyes of flesh and open your eyes of the spirit. See the multitudes that are with you, that knew you were going to be exactly where you are at this precise moment and are there to help you, guide you, support you through God's perfect will and lead you safely through life's many Gateways.

CHARACTERS

Immortals

Guardians

Enoch – Scott's guardian from the guardian clan of writers and visionaries, creators of things unseen. Helped in the inspiration of new ideas.

Israfel - Darnisha's guardian, from the clan of worshipers. An angel of music and inspirer of worship songs to the Lord.

Vohumanah - Jacqueline's guardian. Encourages her to think positive and have optimistic outlook . Transforms negative and worried thoughts .

Shemael - Patrick's guardian. Inspires feelings of gratitude and thankfulness in the heart.

Gavreel – Peggy's guardian. Helps you make peace with enemies. Also encourages mental balance and peace of mind .

Barakiel - Wealthy old businessman's guardian. Angel of financial wisdom and success and worldly favor.

Commanding legion of Wind and Water

Sachiel - was the presiding commander over all waters.

Elemeniah - watched over those who travel on waters.

Azariel - ruled over the winds.

Archangels

Aneal - the archangel of passion and romance.

Jophiel - the keeper of the Book of Life.

The Fallen Immortals

Lucifer – Prince of Darkness, the devil, the fallen angel cast down from heaven.

Dezro – The old scout demon.

Lucifer's minister – The Anti-Christ.

Mortals

Patrick – Jacqueline's husband lives in Beulah on Crystal Lake.

Jacqueline – lives in Beulah with her husband Patrick's. Has owns a custom jewelry shop.

Peggy – Best friend of Jacqueline.

NuWang – Chinese woman from Beijing China. "My Daughter who is a Queen"

Our Angels on Earth

From left to right

Peggie Schwartz, Jackleen & Patrick Carmack

Keep up with Scott Anthony Taylor

Check out the DEATHGATE website at

www.deathgatebook.com

For personal appearances, book signing, and speaking engagements, contact

S.A. Taylor Company
916-997-6309
or email: booking@deathgatebook.com

Follow Scott's blog

Starting over at 40...Making a Life not a Living

www.scottanthonytaylor.posterous.com

Also follow Scott on Facebook

www.facebook.com/scubascotty
or
"Deathgate" by Scott Anthony Taylor

Look for Scott's wife, Darnisha Taylor's, new CD and DVD

PRAISE YOU LIVE

Find them on

Itunes

and

www.darnishataylor.com

DEATHGATE

Coming soon From Scott Anthony Taylor

A new fictional adventure

Also Coming Soon

A Daily Crisis Devotional

Watch for Scott and Darnisha's new vacation and retreat endeavor

Vidurria Luxury Charters

www.vidurria.com

Featuring Romantic, Spiritual
and
Crisis Recovery Cruises